The Perfumed
DEATH

The Perfumed
DEATH

MADELON ST. DENIS

COACHWHIP PUBLICATIONS
GREENVILLE, OHIO

The Author

Very little is known about the author, Madelon St. Denis. The use of 'St. Dennis' on her two traditionally published books appears to be a change by her publisher to accommodate marketing of those titles, as 'St. Denis' was often used on her magazine novels and foreign translations. 'St. Denis' is also how her name appears on a 1930 U.S. Census form, which notes she was born in 1885 in Massachusetts, and had been married at the age of 23. (She was 45 at the time of the census, lodging in New York.) One of her books, *The Death Kiss,* was made into a movie, so her name appears in conjunction with that in the 1930s, but she appears to have stopped writing by the end of the decade.

The Perfumed Death, by Madelon St. Denis
© 2024 Coachwhip Publications edition

First published August 1931, *Complete Detective Novel Magazine*
Book format, 1932 (as *The Perfumed Lure*)
CoachwhipBooks.com

ISBN 1-61646-589-1
ISBN-13 978-1-61646-589-6

1

"Inspector Fisk speaking."

"Conway Fisk, of the Homicide Bureau?"

"Yes."

"This is Dr. Alan Munro. I'm calling to report a death under suspicious circumstances."

"One of your patients?"

"No. A young man named Cyril Kenwick. I was merely called in because I happen to live close by."

Inspector Fisk, after a moment's hesitation, asked for the Kenwick address and receiving it, promised to come immediately.

"You'll wait for us, of course?"

"Surely."

Fisk set down the telephone and turned to the man with whom he had been talking when its insistent ringing cut the thread of their discussion.

"A doctor reporting what he evidently suspects as a case of murder. I'm going up to a place in the east seventies, want to come along?"

"Too busy, or rather too interested in the play I started in last night's wee small hours."

"Sorry." Fisk was straightening papers and locking drawers preparatory to leaving the office. "Even if you're no more than what one might call a dilettante detective I always find an investigation more interesting when you're along."

"Probably because it's not routine work with me," Sydney Traherne answered with a half-smile. "After all I sometimes need a vacation from the strenuous labors of playwriting—"

"Odd idea of a vacation, yours."

"Possibly. Yet isn't a complete change the very essence of a holiday? City dwellers flock to the country and vice versa, just as when the attempt to write sparkling comedy enmeshes me in webs of pessimistic gloom I grasp at the nearest case of death and destruction to rest my mind and cheer me up. But don't let me keep you, we can finish our talk some other time and your doctor's probably counting the seconds till your arrival. Can I give you a lift? My car's outside."

As he spoke two plainclothes men for whom Fisk had rung while they talked, knocked and entered, both greeting Sydney Traherne as an old acquaintance.

"Looks like a murder call," Inspector Fisk briefly explained to them. "Mr. Traherne's driving us up town."

The address furnished by the unknown doctor fitted an old-fashioned house in the lower seventies; a house that sat slightly back from the street which it seemed to regard with a dignified reserve from behind its own small, iron-railed strip of box-bordered lawn. It was larger than the average New York house, probably built in days when land was less prohibitively expensive, so that the front steps led up to a door in its center instead of, as more frequently the case, at the extreme side.

Sydney Traherne's car drew in to the curb and when the inspector and his men had alighted, Conway Fisk renewed his suggestion of cooperation.

"Thanks, but it's probably no more than a felonious entry with intent to rob—this neighborhood and particularly this house, looks much too conservative to harbor a more personal type of murder—besides I've several lines of the new play fairly crying to be put on down on paper. Drop in to-morrow, or whenever you have time, and let me know if my diagnosis happens to be wrong."

As his high-powered car swept smoothly away Inspector Fisk mounted the steps, followed by Nelson and Brady, his two assistants. Their ring was answered by a short, surprisingly chubby butler with an innocently round pink face, now decorated by a look of grieved astonishment.

"You're the police gentlemen?" he inquired in a lugubrious whisper, then, on being assured that they were, led the way on tip-toe toward a half open door on the left of the wide hallway.

Inside was a sedately furnished library, all inset bookcases and leather upholstered, comfortable looking chairs. A tall, slenderly built man, whose handsome dark face rather contradicted the apparent age assigned him by almost snow-white hair, left his position on the hearth and came forward as they entered.

"Inspector Conway Fisk?"

"Yes, and you, I suppose, are Dr. Munro. Do you mind telling us precisely what's happened?"

"Perhaps you'd rather see the body first?" The doctor's hand indicated a couch pushed against the further wall in such a position that its occupant lay in deep shadow. Then, without waiting for the inspector's answer, he crossed to switch on a reading lamp which threw a strong light down on the dead face lying against a leather cushion at the couch's head. It was a young face, well-bred, finely featured, though marked by certain signs of dissipation that could be read even through its now convulsed expression of mortal agony. "Not a pleasant sight," Dr. Munro's voice went on. "That's why Barnabus and I, who've been keeping vigil until you arrived, turned out the reading lamp."

"H-u-m-m," Conway Fisk stood looking down at the boyish face then glanced up at the older man. "Poison?"

"I think so, though apparently one with which I'm entirely unfamiliar. Do you prefer hearing my story, or examining the body first?"

"The latter's a job for the medical examiner," Fisk turned toward his assistants. "Ring him up, will you, Nelson, the butler'll doubtless show you the phone."

As Nelson and the butler departed on their errand Inspector Fisk switched off the reading lamp and led the way back toward the close vicinity of the quietly smoldering fire; for some reason that stiff young figure on the couch lent the big room a certain chill.

"Now, doctor."

"There's not much to tell." The doctor had resumed his former position on the hearth, one arm resting against the mantel. "My office is only two doors away; and perhaps three-quarters of an hour ago some one rang me up to say a doctor was urgently needed at the Kenwicks' house. The voice sounded so agitated that I waited to ask no questions, simply grabbed my bag and dashed here on the run rather imagining there'd been some sort of accident; an emergency case in fact."

"What gave you that impression?"

"If it was ordinary illness they'd naturally call their own physician—whereas in case of accident it would be quite natural to summon the doctor nearest at hand."

"Then these Kenwicks aren't on your list of patients?"

"If you remember, that question was asked and answered over the phone," Dr. Munro reminded him. "As a matter of fact, having lived close by for several years, I knew both father and son by sight but this is the first time I ever entered their home."

"A father, is there? What's become of him, by the way?"

"Retired to his study, he couldn't stand waiting in the same room with his dead son, too harrowing I imagine. The butler, who, so he tells me, boasts the name of 'Barnarbas,' has run in there once or twice to make sure he was all right. I don't know if he notified Mr. Kenwick that you'd arrived."

Apparently the butler had not neglected that duty for as Dr. Munro finished speaking Nelson reentered the room closely followed by a tall, bent-shouldered old gentleman in dressing gown and slippers whose disproportionately small head was sunk in the loose folds of a long, forward-thrust neck, lending him somewhat the effect of a brooding eagle, the more so because his narrow head was smoothly bald. His eyes went first toward the shadowy couch against the wall, then glanced uninterestedly from one strange face to another.

"You're the police, I suppose," the old gentleman's voice was astonishingly deep and melodious, considering the scrawny throat from which it issued. "This doctor—um—I've forgotten his name, insisted on sending for you though I told him there was no necessity. Cyril's simply paid for the error of his ways."

Rather a singular speech, as coming from a recently bereft parent. Conway Fisk stared at him curiously, then remembered the signs of dissipation on the son's boyish face.

"You think he's simply struck some thoroughly poisonous booze?"

Without immediately answering, the old man shuffled forward to sink into a chair and spread two clawlike hands toward the fire.

"No," came the final expression of his opinion. "No. I think the Lord has punished his numerous sins—nothing else."

The answer was unexpected enough to cause a momentary pause, during which the chubby Barnabus slipped quietly into the room, closing the door behind him. The click of its latch caught Fisk's ear, reminding him that the hall remained unguarded. He sent Brady to remedy the omission and at the same time watch for the medical examiner.

"So far Dr. Munro's only had a chance to tell us how he was hurriedly summoned here," the inspector spoke to Mr. Kenwick rather than to Dr. Munro himself. "We've heard nothing about what happened when he arrived. Now that you're here, Mr. Kenwick, we'd better start the story at its beginning—then the doctor can give his evidence in its proper place."

There is no story," Mr. Kenwick stated with a touch of resignation. "Cyril simply came home and—died."

"We'll need to start further back than that," Fisk informed him. "Where had your son been, for instance? or no, better begin with this morning and tell us how he spent the day."

"I've not the shadow of an idea," the old gentleman patiently informed him. "We met for the first time today at mid-day dinner—Cyril was not in the habit of rising early enough to breakfast with me, particularly on a Sunday when my usual hour is pushed forward so that I may attend early service—as I say, we took mid-day dinner together as always on the Sabbath; of course during the remainder of the week we dine at night."

"And was your son quite as usual at that time?"

Mr. Kenwick gave the question deliberate consideration before answering it:

"Quite as usual, I think, save that he was perhaps a trifle more under the influence of liquor than was customary at that hour."

"But he didn't complain of feeling unwell?"

"No, quite the contrary—he appeared so hilarious that I felt called on to remind him such a mood ill befitted the Sabbath day."

"And after dinner, do you know what he did then?"

"As I told you, I've no idea. Possibly Barnabus can say."

"We'll question him later—at present I want your own version of events. When did you next see your son?"

"Soon after I'd finished my solitary supper. He came into this room at about eight o'clock."

"To tell you that he was sick?"

"Not at all—" the old man flatly contradicted. "To tell me that he meant marrying the unspeakable woman with whom he was in love, quite regardless of anything I might say or do to prevent it."

"So?" Fisk's tone held a dash of new interest. "Your son was engaged, was he?"

"If you like to call it that. At any rate he intended marrying a woman of whom he knew I thoroughly disapproved."

"Any special reason?"

"Many."

"We'll take that up a bit later on. For the present better stick to what happened to-night. Your son came into this room at, or about, eight o'clock, at which time he informed you he meant marrying without your consent. And then what happened?"

"I was in the midst of telling Cyril my candid opinion both of the lady and of his own manner of life, when he was suddenly seized by some kind of a frightful illness—he appeared to be in great pain and at the same time the victim of a paralysis that prevented his uttering a sound. I rang for Barnabus and together we managed to get him onto the couch, then Barnabus insisted on calling in a doctor though I felt sure it was useless—my son had plainly been smitten by the avenging hand of God."

Inspector Fisk let the statement pass and turned to Barnabus, quietly waiting on the fringe of the little group.

"Why did you summon Dr. Munro, since I understand he was a complete stranger?"

"I tried first to get Dr. Bell, the family's regular doctor," Barnabus meekly explained. "Then, when they told me he was out of town I called Dr. Munro because he lived in this same block and his name was known to me through seeing it so often in passing by."

"He came at once?"

"Inside of five minutes, I'm sure, sir."

"And what time was this?"

"I can't say to the minute, sir, I only know it was a little after 8:30. I'd heard the hall clock strike the half-hour before Mr. Kenwick rang."

"You brought Dr. Munro in here the instant he arrived?"

"Yes, sir."

"And you, doctor?" He turned to the physician, at the same time signing Barnabus to stay in the room as he had not yet finished questioning him. "Was the patient alive or dead when you first saw him?"

"Dead. Otherwise I might be better able to hazard a guess as to what poison killed him."

"At least you've no doubt it was poison of some kind?"

"Well—" Dr. Munro retired behind a sudden caution. "You doubtless know how we medical men dislike making an unqualified statement on anything less than the most conclusive evidence—but in this case I don't object to saying that to the best of my present belief the lad died from some virulent, though to me unknown, poison."

"The autopsy will doubtless tell us more about it." Fisk spoke with a comfortable assurance born of past experience. "Now, when Barnabus brought you in Mr. Kenwick was alone with the body of his son?"

"Yes."

"You saw no one else?"

"Not a soul."

"Mr. Kenwick was naturally broken-hearted over the boy's sudden death?"

"I suppose so," the doctor's pleasantly cultured voice sounded slightly dubious. "To be quite honest I don't think I paid him much attention. I vaguely remember seeing him kneel near the foot of the couch, and hearing him send up some sort of prayer for the peaceful passing of the boy's soul. I'm afraid I was more interested in the death itself, and afterwards in getting into touch with police headquarters—and you."

"Why did you specify me in particular? I remember your insistence on hearing my full name before you'd part with any information whatever."

"Well," for a second the handsome doctor looked distinctly sheepish, though his frank blue eyes met the inspector's very steadily. "I've a certain theory regarding crime detection which I'd be glad to tell you at some other time—that is if you care to hear it—and the search for confirmatory data leads me into following the printed accounts of various major crimes rather closely. Just recently I've been reading a lot about you in connection with the Baxter murder."

"So that was it. I wondered how you happened to be familiar with my name. Now, one more question, doctor, and we'll listen to whatever Barnabus can tell us concerning how young Kenwick spent the day and early evening. As you came up the block from your own house did you see any one leaving this one?"

"No," Dr. Munro answered after a moment's reflection. "Though I think I should certainly have noticed any one doing so—there happened to be very few passers by."

"You've already told us you saw no one but Mr. Kenwick and Barnabus after entering; I imagine that about finishes your testimony."

"Not quite, inspector, there's one very odd circumstance to which I'd like to call your attention—one for which I can't in the least account—Cyril Kenwick's lips and mouth are perfumed with a most peculiar perfume, a flowery, spicy scent unlike anything I've ever smelled before."

2

When Inspector Fisk had verified the doctor's assertion by stooping over the couch and applying an attentive nose to the dead man's lips and half open mouth, he again switched off the reading lamp and returned to the group clustered near the fire.

"Curious. Do you know of any poison which, if taken into the mouth, would be likely to leave it saturated with that strange scent?"

"None." The doctor's silvered head shook an emphatic denial. "As I've already told you it's utterly unlike anything I've ever before encountered."

"Could it be caused by one of these new home-brewed cordials?"

"And remain as strong as that?" The doctor's dark brows twitched quizzically. "Hardly, I think."

"Better trust the autopsy for an explanation," Fisk decided. "And now, Barnabus, let us have an account of your young master's day—as complete as possible, please."

Thus forced into the limelight the butler's round face became several shades pinker than usual while his chubby features twisted into a look of acute distress; it was one thing to answer direct questions, quite another to volunteer a consecutive narrative.

"Well, sir, I think Mr. Cyril got up at about the same time as always—though I can't personally vouch for the fact, as I'd orders never to disturb him without special instructions—no matter how late he slept. At any rate he came down stairs just before the one o'clock dinner gong sounded."

"Had he no breakfast at all?"

"That I can't say, sir, one of the maids may have carried up some coffee, he seldom took more than that of a morning."

"And, speaking of maids, I suppose you're not the only servant in the house?"

"No, sir, of course not, there's cook and two housemaids; no other manservant."

"Nor housekeeper?"

"No, sir, I've charge of the household, in a manner of speaking."

"Where are they now?"

"Out, sir, it's Sunday night, at which time I always give them the evening off unless we've special company."

"And the family itself consists of?"

"Only Mr. Kenwick and Mr. Cyril, sir. Mrs. Kenwick died more than ten years ago."

"Well, then, to return to your evidence touching how Cyril Kenwick spent his day,—the first time you saw him was just before dinner; go on from there."

"He and his father dined quite as usual, sir; when they'd finished Mr. Kenwick went to his study and Mr. Cyril went out, not leaving word where he was going or when he'd be back though he generally told me one, or both, on account of phone calls while he was gone. He came in again about five o'clock when I happened to be in the front hall, and told me to bring a plate of sandwiches and some wine to his room as quick as I could manage it, as he didn't mean staying home for supper. I had Jessie make the sandwiches and took up the tray myself. Mr. Cyril was changing to the evening clothes he's wearing now and seemed in a goodish hurry, telling me between bites that he'd had as much preaching as he could stomach for one day—begging your pardon, sir"—with an apologetic side glance toward the oddly detached Mr. Kenwick—"and meant going out again before supper time. I came back down stairs and when he'd finished dressing he came to my pantry, saying he could be reached at Mrs. Tabour's in case any one phoned. Then he went out, sir, and that was the last I saw of him until Mr. Kenwick rang and I found Mr. Cyril here in some kind of a seizure."

"You didn't admit him when he came home that last time?"

"No, he'd a latch key and must have let himself in."

"Now, Barnabus, a little while back you said all three maid servants were out, yet afterward mentioned having a certain Jessie put up the sandwiches asked for by Mr. Cyril—is she still another maid, or perhaps a visitor of your own?"

"Neither, sir." Barnabus seemed decidedly scandalized by the latter half of the inspector's question. "You see it's arranged like this—two of the women have leave to go out directly the Sunday dinner dishes are washed up and put away, the third, taking it turn and turn about, stays in and helps me over a cold supper, then she's the rest of the evening off. To-day it was Jessie's turn to give me a hand."

"But she also went out before Mr. Cyril returned?"

"Yes, sir, at about seven-thirty I should think."

"Hum-m, so you and Mr. Kenwick were alone in the house at the moment of Cyril's death." Inspector Fisk retired into a meditative little silence, presently emerging to remark: "A little later I shall want a look at his room. Will you take officer Nelson up there, Barnabus?" Then, to the plainclothes man: "Take a look round, especially at any letters or papers, but don't touch the tray on which wine and sandwiches were served—I'll want a go at that myself, for anything he ate or drank to-day may prove important."

When butler and plainclothes man had left the room Conway Fisk stood for some seconds, staring at the curiously impassive figure in the big leather chair, then he turned to Dr. Munro with a question.

"Has he been so apparently indifferent from the moment of your first entry?"

"Much the same. Probably he's more or less dazed by the sudden loss, though, now I've time to think back, that prayer he put up sounded extremely coherent; it gave no impression of a bewildered or grief-stricken brain behind the lips that framed it."

"Well, dazed or not it's time for him to clear up a few points." The inspector drew a chair close to the one holding the bald-headed old gentleman. "Now, Mr. Kenwick, from other witnesses we've obtained a fairly full account of what happened—perhaps you won't object to further enlightening us. To begin with, was Cyril your only son?"

Slowly the oddly small head stretched up from its encasing folds of scrawny flesh, turning until the close-set beady eyes could stare directly into the inspector's face.

"Only son? Did you ask if Cyril was my only son?"

"I did."

"Of course he was, my only child in fact—didn't his birth make my wife a hopeless invalid, so that she dragged out a miserable existence for ten pain-filled years and finally died when her marvelous courage at last petered out?" His answering voice was nothing less than venomous. "Only God in his infinite wisdom knows how she ever came to have such a son! It's been an increasing mystery to me every year of his life."

"You mean—your son has been something of a disappointment?"

"Disappointment!" The single word sounded like a discordant jeer. "That's a mild way of putting it! Wouldn't you be disappointed if a glorious bird of paradise hatched out a viper?"

"Aren't you forgetting the young man's dead?"

"Neither that nor any of the evil he did while living—my memory's of the best."

Inspector Fisk prudently dropped the subject of Cyril's morals, taking up his reported engagement instead.

"When speaking of the lady your son wanted to marry you told us she was some one of whom you thoroughly disapproved but gave no reason. I'd like to hear what you have against the lady; what's her name, by the bye?"

"Shirley Tabour—Mrs. Shirley Tabour! She's a divorcée, years older than my son and of very questionable virtue. Any wonder I disapproved of the match?"

"Poor?"

"How should I know? Probably not, that type of woman seldom is; not while they're young and passably beautiful at least."

"Can you give me her address?"

"I cannot. I've never visited her, in fact I've never seen her. What I heard was quite enough."

"Slightly unfair to judge the lady purely on hearsay." Fisk was conscious of a growing dislike for the vulture-headed old gentleman. "You might have placed a little reliance on your son's good taste."

"Yes, on matters of dress, not women," came the sneering retort. "Cyril was barely twenty-one but distinctly precocious—I've already bought off several unspeakable females to avoid a scandal. This time I meant letting things take their course with no interference from me."

"How long has he known Mrs. Tabour?"

"That I can't say. The affair only came to my knowledge about a month ago."

Here they were interrupted by the return of Nelson who signaled his chief that he had something to report, a flicker of his eyes toward Mr. Kenwick at the same time appraising Fisk that his news in some way concerned the old man. Before he had time to decide whether or not to drop questioning Mr. Kenwick in favor of hearing Nelson's report, the question was settled by sounds of the medical examiner's arrival.

He came bustling in, very apologetic for having taken so long in answering their call; he had been out when it arrived and was only reached by his assistant who had taken the message, after a good deal of delay. Inspector Fisk introduced Dr. Munro to him, then tried to persuade Mr. Kenwick into leaving the room; a thing he politely but stubbornly refused to do.

The medical examiner turned on the reading lamp and bent over Cyril's body, then asked Dr. Munro precisely what symptoms he had noticed on first arriving and, as the two medical heads drew close together in whispered consultation, Conway Fisk left the room, signing Nelson to follow. In the hall they found Barnabus vaguely hovering about.

"I thought you were both supposed to be keeping an eye on Cyril Kenwick's room, and more especially on the wine and sandwich tray."

"So we were, but as it happens there's nothing there worth watching," Nelson explained. "The tray's gone and what's more, though we looked in both kitchen and pantry, there's no sign of either dishes, decanter or wine glass—they've all vanished into thin air."

"Yes? Now that's a cheerful discovery!" Fisk considered it for a moment, then asked: "Did you use the word 'decanter' advisedly?"

"Sure. Barnabus says he took up a decanter of port."

"Which normally belongs—where?"

"On the dining room sideboard, sir." It was Barnabus who volunteered the answer.

"Either of you look to see if it was back in its proper place?"

"Never thought of it," Nelson admitted. "We were hunting the whole tray."

"Which is the dining room?"

Barnabus opened its door and switched on the lights. Inside was a big somber room with a huge carved sideboard on which sat the missing decanter still half full of wine. When Barnabus had identified it as the one taken up to young Kenwick's room Fisk turned to his assistant with a question that sounded utterly irrelevant.

"Happen to notice if the bed in Cyril's room was turned down for the night?"

"Hanged if I see how the fact hitches up with the missing tray but it was; bedclothes neatly folded back so whoever used the bed'd have no trouble opening it up."

"I imagine we'll find this maid, Jessie, simply saw the soiled plates and glass when she went in to turn down the bed and carried off the whole tray, washing and putting away the used dishes; or are you responsible for the turned down bed, Barnabus?"

"Not me, sir, that's something the maids always attend to."

"Then we'll have to wait till we can question Jessie. In the meantime, why'd you look at Mr. Kenwick, Nelson? Found out anything queer about him?"

"Sort of. Barnabus and I got to talking while we trailed the vanished tray—he tells me Mr. Kenwick hated his son."

"That's a strong statement, my man. Sure it's accurate?"

The butler's round eyes met his unwaveringly. "Indeed there was never any secret about it, sir," he declared. "I didn't come here until after Mrs. Kenwick died; but cook, who's been with the family for fifteen years, tells me Mrs. Kenwick was a saint on earth and her husband fair worshiped her—he never forgave the son because his birth cost the mother her health."

"He's certainly shown no signs of strong parental affection to-night." The news did not seem to surprise Fisk.

"Not to-night or ever, sir. It was the way his father treated him that made young Cyril so wild, I've always thought." Barnabus' aggrieved tone revealed that he had harbored a certain affection for the irresponsible son of the house. "Why, even to-night I heard the old man say he'd sooner see Mr. Cyril dead than married to Mrs. Tabour."

"When was this?" Fisk showed sudden interest.

"It must have been soon after Mr. Cyril came home and went in the library, sir. Happening to pass the shut door I heard Mr. Kenwick shouting at the top of his lungs—and he's a strong pair as you may have noticed just in hearing him speak—first, like I told you, he said he'd rather see Mr. Cyril dead than married to that 'slut' was the word he used, I think. Then he up and called for the vengeance of the Lord to punish the lad's sinful ways."

"And this scene occurred during the last half hour of Cyril's life," Inspector Fisk reflected aloud. "You didn't stay to hear how it ended."

"No, sir. I've always disliked hearing the old gentleman shout and call down curses from heaven. I'm not an overly religious man myself, but such goings-on strike me as blasphemous. I went to my pantry and stayed there till I was rung for."

"H-u-m. Too bad Jessie took it on herself to wash up that tray service so promptly—there's a chance of this proving an inside job. Now, Barnabus, I'd like Mrs. Tabour's address." Fisk took out his watch and glanced at the time. "Not yet eleven. Think I'll pay the lady a visit, that is if she doesn't live too far away."

"Only a couple of blocks, sir, around on Park Avenue." The butler gave him the exact address and apartment number, both of which he knew through transmitting phone messages to various friends of young Kenwick's.

"Ah, the address more or less answers my question as to whether the lady's poor." He indicated the decanter of port on the sideboard. "Take charge of that, Nelson, and have its contents analyzed, though I doubt there being anything wrong with it; if there was, the decanter would most probably have been either emptied or smashed." He started for the door. "I'm leaving you and Brady in charge here while I'm gone."

In the front hall Dr. Munro was just preparing to leave the house. "There seems no way in which I can assist," he told the inspector, "and the library's pretty well crowded with various men from headquarters, photographers, fingerprint experts and so forth. I admit hating to leave,—the whole process is thrillingly interesting to a person who's never before seen the machinery of the law at work—but the medical examiner made it more or less plain that a mere outsider was de-trop."

"I'm just starting to visit the lady young Kenwick was anxious to marry," Inspector Fisk informed him. "Why not come along? It's quite possible she will need a doctor's care when I break the news of Cyril's death."

"That's thundering kind of you, inspector." The doctor's tone was warmly grateful. "I don't mind admitting that I'm simply eaten by curiosity—and the thing that fascinates me most is seeing precisely how you set about unraveling the sorry tangle."

3

Shirley Tabour received them in a room all French gilt and pale pink and blue; a color scheme that rather accurately matched her own radiant but distinctly artificial beauty of eyes and complexion.

Inspector Fisk had only sent up word that he needed to see her on urgent business connected with young Cyril Kenwick, so that news of the latter's death came as a decided shock. Under it she cried out sharply; a cry that was instantly answered by the entrance of another woman who must have been waiting in the adjoining room.

The new comer was of about Shirley Tabour's own age, somewhere in the later twenties, but of a very different type. Rather tall, slender, golden-brown eyed and chestnut haired. Shirley clutched at her in hysterical despair.

"Fay, oh, Fay—isn't it horrible?—and to think how I abused the poor dear only this afternoon!"

"You're forgetting I don't know what's wrong." The woman addressed as "Fay" patted the weeping Shirley soothingly, while she glanced from Inspector Fisk to the doctor. It was the former who answered her inquiring look.

"Young Mr. Kenwick died, very suddenly, a little over two hours ago. We came, partly to break the news to Mrs. Tabour, partly to ask if she can tell us anything about his movements during this afternoon and early evening."

"Oh, I can't—can't talk about him!" Shirley Tabour sobbed wildly. "Please go away, I'd rather be alone with Fay."

"Sorry to seem disobliging," Fisk betrayed no intention of obeying the request. "Better have a look at her, Dr. Munro, it's necessary for us to know what she has to tell as soon as possible."

With the help of the serene-eyed lady of the chestnut hair Dr. Munro succeeded in getting Shirley Tabour to swallow a dose of aromatic spirits of ammonia; after which she showed signs of a restored interest in her own appearance, an always hopeful symptom with women of her type. Only a few minutes later she had sufficiently recovered to sit erect and dab a discreet handkerchief at one severely damaged eye.

"If you'll just sit down and have a little patience I'll go and bathe my face," she presently declared. "Fay dear, please ask Alice to make some coffee—or perhaps the gentlemen would prefer something stronger." She drifted away, bent on repairing the ravages wrought by unchecked indulgence in real tears.

"Shirley forgot to give you my name so I'd better introduce myself. I'm her cousin, Mrs. Redmond," the brown-eyed woman explained as the door closed behind Mrs. Tabour. "Won't you really make yourselves comfortable?" Then, to the trim maid who answered her hand on the bell: "Coffee, Alice, please, very strong coffee." She had ignored Shirley Tabour's suggestion of a less temperate stimulant.

When the hostess returned a scant ten minutes later she had quite regained her self-control and seemed ready to answer whatever questions the inspector chose to put.

"I understand from Mr. Kenwick that you and his son were engaged," he commenced as Shirley settled into a becoming attitude on the fragile little pink couch.

"So we were, until this afternoon when we quarreled—"

"I'm afraid I'll have to ask you what about."

"Is that necessary?"

"Quite."

"Then,—well it was because Cyril found out I'd been seeing something of Jerome and fussed about it. So unreasonable, don't you think? objecting to a girl's lunching with her own husband!"

"Husband?" Fisk repeated, puzzled as to how a woman could possess both husband and fiancé at the same time.

"Oh, well, ex-husband of course, if you insist on being literal." Shirley pouted at him with a hint of reproach. "Anyway Jerome and I've always stayed the best possible friends even if we did tire of sharing a matrimonial yoke. I can't see that it was any business of Cyril's."

"He was jealous of Mr. Tabour, perhaps?"

"Oh, unquestionably! And the awful part was Jerome returned the sentiment—with interest! So inconvenient, wasn't it? and terribly inconsistent—when he didn't like me as a wife himself why object to my marrying somebody else?"

"Was this—er—objection, an active emotion?"

"Oh, dear, yes! I had a scene with Jerome only yesterday, probably that's why the one with Cyril about him acted as a sort of last straw and made me break our engagement. I really meant it, too, though Cyril insisted calling me 'peevish' and said I'd feel differently by to-morrow."

"The trouble happened this afternoon, I think you said?"

"Did I? Well I wasn't very truthful then; it was at cocktail time, somewhere along between six and seven, or possibly just a trifle later."

"Let me get this straight, please." The inspector was making entries in a note book he had fished out as soon as they settled to actual questions and answers. "At what hour to-day did you first see Cyril Kenwick?"

"It's so difficult to be certain of exact times." Shirley gave the impression of a natural mental vagueness rather than a deliberate attempt at evasion. "It was after six, I know that, because when Fay phoned to ask if I'd like having her for dinner to-night she mentioned it was six o'clock then and she'd be here about seven. I don't quite know how soon after that Cyril came, but it wasn't very long, and he already knew about my seeing Jerome for he started fussing before we'd had our second cocktail."

"Well, shall we put it that your quarrel took place somewhere between six and seven?" Inspector Fisk patiently suggested. "Perhaps you can say what time young Kenwick left here?"

"Heavens! you do expect a woman to be a regular alarm clock, don't you? I haven't the least idea what time he left."

"It was at a quarter to eight, exactly," Fay Redmond quietly volunteered.

"You're sure of that?" The inspector turned to her with an air of decided relief.

"Yes. Alice let me in a few minutes after seven, she didn't tell Shirley I'd come because we both heard her quarreling with Cyril. I went back through the dining room and waited about, meaning to keep out of sight till he'd gone. That's why I noticed the precise time. I kept glancing at my watch as one does when waiting for some one to go."

"A quarter to eight," the inspector thoughtfully repeated. "Then he must have gone directly home, for his father saw him at eight o'clock and there'd be just about time to make the distance if he walked. Did he usually do that?"

"Always, unless it was storming," Shirley reentered the conversation. "Walking the few blocks between our homes was easier than taking a taxi and following one way arrows all over Robin Hood's Barn. But why are you asking so many questions? and you haven't told us what happened to Cyril after he left here?"

"I'll explain that a bit later on," Fisk hedged, anxious to obtain as much information as possible before either woman guessed it a case of probable murder. "I take it, you and Cyril Kenwick were alone during what you call the cocktail hour? You had no other visitors?"

"No one else for a wonder—generally there's more or less of a crowd."

"And you hadn't seen him earlier in the day?"

"No. Yesterday he suggested a drive this afternoon, but to-day he didn't turn up till somewhere around six—as I've already told you."

"He didn't mention what he'd done instead of taking you for the proposed ride?"

"No." Shirley's brilliantly golden head shook dissentingly. "He said nothing about how he'd spent the day—simply started right in fussing about Jerome."

"Now, just one more question and I'll leave you in peace," Fisk had begun, when the maid reentered with a laden coffee tray; he promptly took advantage of her presence as she arranged the service on a table close to Shirley's elbow, by asking: "Did you wash up the cocktail shaker and glasses used before dinner tonight?"

"Why yes, sir, of course." The girl eyed him with open surprise before slipping quietly from the room.

"Why this keen interest in my household arrangements?" Shirley Tabour wanted to know. "And what was the question you'd started to ask me when Alice came in?"

"I put it to her instead. You see, Cyril Kenwick was poisoned, therefore anything he ate or drank today naturally becomes important."

"Poisoned!" Both women echoed the dread word with a touch of horror.

"You don't mean—" Shirley leaned toward him, the color draining from her face so that the rouge stood out in ghastly looking patches. "You can't mean he was—murdered?"

"I'm afraid so, unless the quarrel with you drove him to suicide."

"That's ridiculous! He didn't take it very seriously and besides he never cared enough. Cyril—murdered—it just doesn't seem possible!"

The inspector had rather feared another outbreak of violent grief, but Shirley Tabour was shocked, or perhaps frightened, into an almost frozen calm.

"Of course we're anxious to learn precisely what food or drink passed his lips within the last few hours. Did he have anything here except the cocktails you've already mentioned?"

"Nothing else, and I mixed them myself, there couldn't have been anything wrong with them for I drank as many as he did."

"And that was?"

"Heavens, what a passion you have for exact numbers and times! I don't quite remember how many, though I don't think it was more than three or four, just possibly five."

"He ate nothing at all?"

"Not so much as a cracker."

"Too bad the shaker and glasses have been washed since then; instant cleaning of china and glassware appears to have become a habit in this case."

On the way back to the Kenwick house, Inspector Fisk paused so suggestively before the one wearing Dr. Munro's neat medical plate that the latter was almost forced into saying a reluctant goodnight and entering it; leaving Fisk free to go on alone.

News of the tragedy had mysteriously spread in the way such news has a habit of doing, and a good-sized group of the merely idly curious was gathered on the sidewalk before the Kenwick house. On the steps themselves clustered a knot of reporters, with difficulty kept at bay by a uniformed officer.

At sight of the inspector they instantly pounced on him, opening fire with a volley of questions, to all of which he turned a cheerfully deaf ear.

"Nothing for publication at the moment, boys," he told them, pushing a good-natured way toward the guarded portal. "Meet me at headquarters in a couple of hours and I'll give you what facts I can."

"That'll be too late for the midnight set-up," somebody aggrievedly protested.

"Can't be helped, I've nothing to say now. Have your paper keep a head line and column open till the last possible instant. Sorry, boys, that's the best I can do."

The door, which had been cautiously opened to admit him, closed in their disgusted faces with a decisive snap.

In the now brightly lighted hall were several men from headquarters; the medical examiner among them.

"Puzzling case, Fisk." He was already hat in hand, ready for departure. "I've sent the body down to the mortuary and we'll do a post mortem in the morning, maybe that will tell us something; so far I can't pin a name to the poison used. Happen to notice the peculiar perfume clinging to his mouth and lips?"

"Yes. Dr. Munro, the doctor they sent for when the boy was taken sick, called my attention to it."

"It's a sickly sort of smell, yet pleasant in a way—unlike anything I ever met before. Wonder what it means?"

"That's for you medical men to determine," the inspector's tone was suddenly brusque; he had just discovered a small seated figure that shrank unobtrusively into the concealing depths of a not-too-distant chair. "How the devil did *you* get in?" he wanted to know.

"Me?" Seeing that she was observed, the girl came meekly forward, a meekness utterly belied by the whole cast of her quaintly impertinent little face, in which everything that could, tilted upward; soft red mouth corners; small saucy nose; big black eyes—even the dainty, close-fitting ears ended in up-pointed tips. "Me? Oh, I just happened to hear there was something going on."

"Happened!" Fisk indulged in a vengeful snort. "When I have time I mean tracing that leak at headquarters—the leak that lets you cheerfully turn up on the scene of a crime before any other reporter gets a smell of anything in the wind."

"Simply feminine intuition, Inspector dear." The girl's big black eyes danced at him, completely unimpressed. "Or if you prefer calling it mental telepathy I've no objection to the term."

"I purpose calling a spade a spade! You've got round somebody at headquarters, and I mean finding out who it is. Not that I blame the poor devil," he added with a sudden relenting. "You've a way with you that would charm a thrush off a hawthorn bush—"

"Well, now that I *am* here, I'd love knowing what the medical examiner meant about that queer perfumy smell in the dead man's mouth. 'Perfumed Death'—heavily leaded—don't you think it'll make a corking headline?"

"Let me catch you using it and I'll wring that impudent neck of yours!" Fisk threatened. "Now, listen, Zoe Panza, I've told the boys to meet me at headquarters in a couple of hours—come along with them and you'll get the details."

"I'll be there," she promised, fishing a small crush hat from her coat pocket and pulling it well down over the delicate, pointed ears. "But I've already enough material for a few scare headlines, have to turn them in first and I'll see you later, Inspector, dear." She made for the door, entirely unmindful of the rumbled threat he sent after her.

"Grab another scoop for that rag of a paper of yours and I'll—I'll—" The dire consequence was lost in the slam of the heavy front door.

4

"But my dear Fisk, the post mortem must have told the doctors *something*," Sydney Traherne's voice sounded ever so slightly bored.

"Well, it didn't," the inspector flatly contradicted. "Or at any rate nothing that served any other purpose than to still further deepen the obscurity. The medical examiner insists the poison that killed Cyril Kenwick was injected into his blood—the doctor who afterwards verified his findings claims that's impossible because there's no trace of a recent skin-puncture anywhere on the body."

"Thinks it was administered in something young Kenwick ate or drank?"

"Rather of that opinion—and the devilish part of it is we can't attempt to check his theory until the stomach contents have been thoroughly analyzed, because every one connected with the case was seized by a perfect mania for dish-washing; they cleaned things up almost before Cyril finished using them."

"Have you traced his movements through that day and the one preceding it?"

"Yes, with the exception of an hour on Sunday afternoon. Saturday's entirely accounted for. Then, Sunday morning we know the Kenwicks' maid, Jessie, took him up some coffee when he rang for it at about eleven o'clock.

Next came dinner—the china used in serving it was all nicely polished long before I came on the scene, but I've had all the foodstuffs left over, analyzed, and the report says nothing wrong with them. After that Cyril went for a walk in the park, several friends who saw and spoke to him there came forward yesterday, after reading the printed accounts of his death, but none of them saw him after about 3:15 at the latest. Between that time and five o'clock when the butler says he returned home, there's a lapse that so far we haven't been able to bridge. Then we have the cocktails drunk with Shirley Tabour—the glassware again carefully cleaned up. The ingredients from which the aforesaid cocktails were mixed have all been analyzed except the orange juice of which there wasn't any left over—same result, nothing in the least out of the way."

"Bit discouraging, isn't it?" Traherne's strong flexible fingers busied themselves over filling a favorite pipe; a proceeding which the inspector watched with a gleam of hopeful interest, knowing that when his friend sought counsel of a pipe rather than a more casual cigarette it was apt to be because the subject under discussion had touched the latent curiosity that often slumbered, quite ungetatable, far down in the depths of his fertile brain.

"How about motive?" Traherne inquired when the pipe was finally drawing to his satisfaction. "Any enlightening glimmers along that line?"

"Nothing startling. Shirley's ex-husband, Jerome Tabour, seems the only one we can tabulate as possessing a half reasonable motive; and when I say 'half' I'm rather stretching it. Hardly seems plausible to accuse a man who divorced Shirley three years ago—it was his doing you know, not hers—of now working up a case of jealousy strong enough to end in murder. Besides I can't see that he'd an opportunity."

"Could he have introduced the poison into Shirley's apartment without her knowledge; say by way of the orange juice or a glass Cyril especially favored?"

"Jerome Tabour never went there," was the inspector's discouraging answer. "Only met his ex-wife for an occasional luncheon or tea."

"Well, opportunity aside, I can't make his motive seem convincing. How about the father? You say Barnabus reports him as hating the boy."

"More resentful of his existence, I imagine, because it had cost the mother her health and eventually her life. But when this so-called hatred let the lad live twenty-one years, it doesn't seem probable it would suddenly flare into a homicidal blaze."

"Not unless some extra fuel was recently added. Your story's passed rather lightly over Kenwick senior; what type is he?"

"Unpleasant old party both mentally and physically. He's the smallest head I ever remember seeing on any full-grown human and the longest, scrawniest neck; looks like a sleepy old vulture brooding over his wrongs."

"Sounds a handsome old dear," Traherne laughed. "Any equally disagreeable mental qualities?"

"Worse if anything. He's a religious fanatic, the actively rabid sort, so much so that the investigation into the cause of his son's death leaves him completely indifferent, he simply insists it was the hand of God that struck Cyril down and no human agency."

Sydney Traherne digested the statement for a silent moment or two, then asked:

"And he violently objected to Cyril's marrying Shirley Tabour?"

"Yes, seems to consider her the last word in depravity."

"So? He looked on the proposed marriage as a sort of climax to the error of Cyril's ways, then. Doesn't it strike you that the key to your problem may lie there? It's possible, just possible mind you, that the old gentleman felt himself the destined instrument of the Lord."

"In other words felt it his duty to end Cyril's career of sin, incidentally ending his life at the same time."

"Fanatics, religious or otherwise, have been known to commit just such insane crimes," Traherne quietly pointed out.

"Then, if the key really does lie there—can't I persuade you into fitting it to the necessary lock?"

"Not a chance." His friend's singular eyes smiled at him, even while the brindled gray and black head shook a firm refusal. "I deserted Boston in favor of New York for the express purpose of leaving friends and fascinating criminal cases in my home city, while I buried myself in the serious business of playwriting. It would take a whole series of eccentric crimes to make me desert my newest comedy."

"Oh, daddy, look how funny that lady's sat down!"

The child's shrill treble apparently failed to penetrate his father's accustomed ears; but it, and his small pointing finger, drew the eyes of several fellow passengers to the rear platform of the subway train, where a stilt-heeled slipper and silken-clad ankle could be seen sticking out into the light from the main passageway at a most unnatural angle.

A man sitting halfway down the car either owned a larger bump of curiosity, or a keener sense of civic duty than the others, for he took it upon himself to investigate.

In the extreme corner of the darkened rear platform of the downtown express a girl lay huddled in a way suggesting that she had slipped down from an upright position after losing consciousness, rather than been overcome by faintness, and sat down of her own accord.

Two men passengers carried her into the lighted car, laying her down stretched full length on a strip of the straw seat hastily vacated for the purpose. She was young, not more than nineteen or twenty, and under ordinary circumstances must have been about averagely pretty—at the moment her face wore a look of blended pain and terror that robbed it of all-natural charm.

"Somebody better page the train for a doctor and call the guard," the passenger who had first risen to investigate that oddly obtrudant little foot suggested.

As it happened there was a physician in the next car and after only the briefest of examinations he pronounced the girl past help—she was already dead.

"Poisoned, I think."

At the word the listening guard's ears pricked attentively and he took instant charge of affairs.

"Sorry to trouble all you people, but this car's got to be sidetracked at 145th street till we can fetch an ambulance and the police," he announced. "I expect the poor kid's done herself in with poison but the police'll need to be sure. They'll want to question all you folks and take your names and addresses; sorry, but it can't be helped."

Calmly following his program in spite of various protests over the delay, car number 99768 was duly backed onto one of the vacant side tracks just below 145th street station, and its passengers detained until the police could arrive and question them.

The process threw no light whatever on the girl's death. Only one susceptible youth remembered seeing her get on at the Van Cortlandt Park station, and he was sure there had been no one with her. No one else had noticed the girl at all, and while all the seats were taken the car had not been sufficiently crowded to drive any other passenger out onto the rear platform.

The young hopeful whose remark had first called attention to the tragedy insisted that he had seen a second girl come in from the back platform and pass through the car at 181st street, just before he noticed the girl's outthrust foot, but no one corroborated his statement and the police showed a disinclination to take it seriously.

It was not until the following morning that Conway Fisk heard of the body found in the subway train, then he received a somewhat cryptic call from the morgue.

"Something here you'd better come down and have a look at; we've an idea it's connected with a case you're working on."

"Man, woman, or child?"

"Come on down and see."

So far the girl remained unidentified. There was nothing in her purse to indicate either name or address, and her clothes were of a cheap ready-made type, carrying no label, other than the original manufacturer's.

Inspector Fisk stood looking down at the pathetic slip of young womanhood spewed by the fantastic city onto so chill a resting place.

"Too bad." There was pity in both his eyes and voice. "She's only a kid!" Then, shaking off the sympathy which, if indulged, would have rendered his profession a much too harrowing affair, he turned to the morgue official who had telephoned him.

"Looks like poison. Suicide I suppose."

"Maybe," the aforesaid official stood rocking from toes to heels, thumbs casually hooked in his opened coat, "and again, maybe not. She was found, dead, on the back platform of a downtown subway express."

"Proving—what?"

"Nothing in particular, only it's a queer, uncomfortable kind of place for a suicide to pick."

The Perfumed Death

"Well, even if it's a case of murder, which you seem to be trying to insinuate, what's it to do with me? I've already got my hands full."

"Not too full," his friend predicted. "Have a smell at the girl's mouth."

After a startled glance Fisk complied, straightening with a smothered oath.

"The same damned perfume that clung to Cyril Kenwick's lips!"

"It is the same then, is it? Of course I only wondered, having read accounts of what the papers call the 'Perfumed Death.' I got curious as soon as I noticed that peculiar spicy kind of odor in the girl's mouth. Only one doctor's looked her over so far and he says it's a case of poisoning, but can't give a name to the one used."

"Neither can anybody else," Fisk bitterly retorted. "The headquarters doctors are fighting like a bunch of drunken tabby-cats over what killed Cyril Kenwick, but they can't even agree whether the stuff was injected or taken internally, much less decide on its infernal name." He hesitated a second, then added gravely: "Jim, that perfume's not the only point of similarity—see here."

Lifting the girl's left hand he pointed to an ordinary rubber band loosely wrapped round the third finger.

"Young Kenwick wore one exactly like that, twisted round the third finger in exactly the same casual way. When I first saw his body the thing made little or no impression, I've often seen nervous people play with an elastic band while talking, wrapping it round one or two fingers, sometimes crossing it into a sort of cat's cradle—I supposed Cyril had been doing something of the kind—but finding the precise duplicate on this girl's finger lifts the rubber ring outside the realm of pure chance. I'll admit coincidence plays queer tricks, but I doubt its leaving two poison victims with a bit of elastic twisted round their third fingers."

"About clinches the girl's connection with the Kenwick case, I'll say," Jim interestedly agreed. "Want the body sent up for autopsy or had she better stay here on the chance of somebody's recognizing her?"

"Keep her here, by all means, and station a reliable man to watch if any visitor recognizes her without reporting the fact. Meanwhile I'd like a look at her purse and clothes."

They told him nothing, however, or almost nothing. The purse held only the usual coin purse, bill fold, handkerchief, and even more necessary compact—the bright blue hat, dress, and thin spring coat were equally uncommunicative; ditto with slippers, stockings and flimsy silks that belonged next the skin; in fact only the girl's white silk slip in the least interested Inspector Fisk. It was cut and gored in a way to make it fit the figure closely, round necked, and entirely devoid of trimming.

"Now that's unlike the straight, shapeless slips one sees flaunting their attractions in every third window," he remarked, eying it curiously. "Wonder why it's cut like that and why it doesn't boast even a scrap of lace or embroidery?"

"Ask some woman," his friend Jim advised.

"I will, but there's not one likely to prove an authority on woman's undies available at the moment."

"There you're wrong. I saw Zoe Panza drifting down a corridor just before you turned up. If she's still in the building she'll be able to enlighten us."

"Damn that kid, she's always under my feet!" the inspector complained, but nevertheless allowed the ubiquitous Zoe to be searched for and finally brought to his friend's office. One glance of her big, tip-tilted eyes was enough to rob the slip of its mystery.

"Why it's the sort of thing wholesale models wear under the dresses or suits they slip on to show customers," she instantly explained. "If it belongs to the Subway Victim of our Perfumed Death she was a dress model to a moral certainty."

"Now who in hell told you anything about a connection between Cyril Kenwick and this unknown female?" the exasperated inspector wrathfully demanded.

"I've got a nose, haven't I?" she cheerfully retorted. "May not be much in the way of an ornament but as a smeller there's nothing wrong with it. Naturally I recognized that nice flowery scent the instant I bent over the girl."

"That leak again!" he groaned.

"Leak nothing—keeping an eye on the morgue's part of my regular beat. Just wait till you read this afternoon's article in my paper!"

She was out the door before Fisk could give adequate expression to his outraged feelings.

Returning to headquarters he sent one of his most trusted men to keep an eye on the morgue and trail any one betraying a secret interest in the unknown girl, then set the police machinery to work canvassing the city's wholesale dress and suit manufactures in search of a missing model.

5

"Dr. Alan Munro. Now who on earth is he?" Shirley Tabour eyed the conservative little visiting card rather blankly. "I'm certain I never heard the name before."

"Isn't he the doctor who came with Inspector Fisk to tell you about Cyril's death?" her cousin asked after an instant's reflection.

"Haven't the slightest idea," Shirley declared. "But let's see him on the chance of your being right; that man's name didn't register at all but I *do* remember thinking him ever so handsome."

"You *would,* regardless of how many corpses decorated the immediate scenery!"

"Don't be catty, Fay dear, it's not my fault if I like attractive men; a compliment they seem pretty willing to return."

"I've never felt the slightest doubt that you sat up in your cradle and flirted with everything in trousers entering your range of vision," Fay retorted with an amused but half-vexed laugh. "Have the handsome doctor in by all means, it'll never do to let your offensive weapons grow rusty from disuse and you've hardly seen any one but the inspector these last few days. I'll go out and cast a motherly eye over the new maid's preparations for dinner."

"You'll do nothing of the kind! You'll stay right here and play propriety. Haven't some of the papers shown a longing to rather frazzle my poor little reputation?"

She sent the hall boy who had brought up Dr. Munro's card to say that, while not receiving ordinary visitors on account of her bereavement, she thought an exception might be made in his case.

"I feel that we're more than mere casual acquaintances," she told him as he bowed over her plump, beautifully manicured hand with a grace that was most distinctly un-American. "Having you here when I first learned Cyril's awful fate, constitutes a sort of bond between us, don't you think?"

"I shall be most happy if you'll continue to regard my visit in that kindly light." Dr. Munro apparently failed to see her inviting pat on the pink cushions beside her and carefully settled himself in a position yielding an uninterrupted view of Fay Redmond. "All this week I've been longing to call. I even tried to smuggle myself in under Inspector Fisk's wing, but he turned a deaf ear to my hints and continued coming alone."

"He's a thrilling sort of creature, so exactly what a ruthless man-hunter ought to be, but all the same I'm afraid of him," Shirley confided with a realistic shiver of arms and shoulders left bare by her somewhat frank negligee. "He's too polite to say so, but I've a dreadful feeling that he suspects me of being responsible for Cyril's death."

"Nonsense, Shirley, he's only upset because your maid so mysteriously disappeared the very night of the murder." Fay Redmond spoke for the first time since the doctor's entry and as if he had been awaiting a signal he instantly transferred his entire attention to her, quite ignoring Shirley's pained cry:

"Please! please! don't use that frightful word, murder— you know how it upsets me!"

"I hadn't heard about the maid's disappearing, the papers have said nothing about it; nor has Inspector Fisk."

"You've seen him, then?"

"Only twice. Once we happened to meet as he was leaving the Kenwick house; once I was asked to consult with the doctor who performed the autopsy on Cyril Kenwick's body. They hoped that, seeing him so short a time after death, I might have noticed some symptom that would help them decide on the poison used."

"Oh dear, won't you people stop talking horrors?" Shirley broke in petulantly. "My nerves simply can't stand much more!"

With an obvious effort Dr. Munro dragged his eyes from enthralled study of Fay's less assertive but more satisfying beauty, to fix them on his hostess's slightly flamboyant charms.

"A thousand pardons, dear Mrs. Tabour, the whole mystery has so ravished my interest that I forget its tragic aspect touches you so nearly. I suppose you'll never forgive me if I beg for further details about your missing maid?"

She felt a certain unwillingness to answer that it was quite all right so long as she, not Fay, supplied them, but the doctor gathered as much from the way she instantly plunged into the story of her maid's heartless desertion at the very moment when her services were most needed.

"Packed her bag and incidentally one of mine, and walked off after we'd gone to sleep Sunday night," she indignantly told him. "Such fiendish ingratitude, when I've been as kind as a sister to that girl! I don't know what on earth I should have done only luckily Joel's out of town so Fay has stayed to see me through the worst."

"Joel?" He questioningly repeated the unfamiliar name.

"Yes, Joel Redmond. Oh, of course you don't know, but he's Fay's husband, a perfectly dried stick of a man old enough to be her father, or probably her grandfather as a matter of fact. There, Fay darling, you needn't 'Hush' me, you know what I say's absolutely true. And the beast simply loathes me, I can't think why, most men don't— even though Fay's my own cousin and we've always been perfectly devoted, he won't let her so much as see me; not with his consent, that is."

"What a shame to try and separate close relations like that!" Dr. Munro prudently sympathized, though in his heart he quite understood Joel Redmond's objection to his wife's association with the fair Shirley. "I hope he's out of town a good deal?"

"More than half the time. He owns factories and things all over this state and two or three others. Fortunately they require constant nursing so Fay and I spend lots of time together. If she hadn't been here now, to see about replacing Alice with a new maid and
generally keep a hand on the helm I'm certain I should have collapsed under the strain."

"Did the girl steal anything, or simply melt away carrying her own belongings?" Dr. Munro made no secret of his consuming interest in anything that touched the Kenwick murder case even remotely.

"Nothing but one of my suitcases, I suppose so she could take nearly all her clothes," his hostess explained, adding with a flash of unexpected shrewdness: "The trouble is her going off like that, so suddenly, makes the police half suspect I've bribed her to stay out of the way because she knows something about how Cyril was poisoned. It isn't true, of course, but you can see how her disappearance gives that impression."

"They'll soon realize their mistake," he consoled.

"Wish I was sure of it—a girl living alone does so hate being sort of watched by the police." Her voice held a much more sincere note than was usual. "If only they'd discover what really did kill Cyril. Personally I shall always believe it was nothing but bad booze—he was terribly careless about what he drank, and who with."

"Then—" Dr. Munro glanced from one woman to the other, doubting the wisdom of proceeding; then abruptly decided on taking the plunge. "Since you mention the possibility of young Kenwick's death being the result of bad liquor I imagine you haven't seen the afternoon papers."

"No, we haven't, and Inspector Fisk hasn't been near us all day. What's happened now?"

"I'd sooner you read the latest development for yourselves—let me get the paper I left with my hat and stick."

Neither of the cousins spoke as he hurried out into the entrance foyer, almost instantly returning, newspaper in hand. It contained Zoe Panza's thrilling account of the dead girl found in the West Side Subway, and, while not literally asserting a connection between her death and that of a well-known youth killed by some as yet unnamed poison, so skillfully suggested a similarity that only the most stupid of readers could overlook the more than hinted link.

"How ghastly!" Fay Redmond's voice held genuine sympathy as she looked up from the printed page which the cousins had read together. "Think of a child like that dying all alone, on a subway train of all hideous places!"

Shirley seemed more curious than horrified. "Do you suppose—but no, I ought not to say that when the girl's dead."

"It's better to be quite frank at a time like this," Dr. Munro urged. "Please tell us what you started to say."

"Only that—well, I always rather wondered if Cyril didn't play round. Do you think this girl could have been a friend of his?"

"Shirley! How can you? When the poor boy utterly adored you!"

"Oh, that." Her lifted shoulders spoke volumes. "I sort of dazzled him, being older and more experienced, but he wasn't ever altogether sure of himself with me—there might easily have been others."

Fay's golden-brown eyes flashed indignantly. "I think it's a shame to suggest it! Besides the paper says she was poorly, or at least cheaply dressed; Cyril would hardly be likely to know a girl of that class."

"Never any telling with a man," her cousin cynically asserted, "the dear things do so love variety."

"Beg pardon, M'am." A very much flustered maid had suddenly appeared in the open doorway. "There's an old gentleman here, I don't know how ever he got up, but he won't take 'no' to seeing you, M'am."

"Tell him I'm not receiving—" Shirley had begun when the maid was unceremoniously brushed aside and David Kenwick stalked into the room, looking more than ever like a badly disgruntled vulture. He took not the slightest notice of Dr. Munro, but stationed his ungainly height in the center of the room, his long neck craning toward first one woman, then the other.

"Which of you is Shirley Tabour?"

"I am," she told him with a touch of meekness; after all he was rather an appalling vision, especially as she had not the remotest idea who he was.

"YOU!" Dr. Munro felt uncertain whether the old man's voice or eyes expressed the more bitter contempt. "If it had been the other one I might have pardoned him, but to love a tinseled counterfeit! Bah! it's small wonder the Lord struck him down!" And without another word or glance he turned, to stalk out of the room.

"Tinseled counterfeit!" Shirley Tabour gasped, a prey to almost inarticulate rage. "The—the filthy old buzzard—how dare he force himself in here and insult me? I'll—I'll call the police!"

"What's that about our honored force?" Inspector Fisk's broad-shouldered figure loomed in the doorway so lately vacated by the equally tall, but bible-backed form of old Mr. Kenwick. "Was it us you were hauling over the coals, by any chance? I only caught your tone, not the words—and wasn't that David Kenwick who brushed past me in the hall?"

"It was," Dr. Munro told him quietly, while Shirley continued to splutter wrathfully.

"So that was Cyril's father! The old beast came in and insulted me. I was threatening to sic the police on him."

"We're already keeping him under a fatherly eye," the inspector assured her. "Knowing his sentiments, why'd you let him come up?"

"I didn't, he simply pranced in unannounced, just as you did. There's certainly something gone wrong with this building to-day, they're letting up every Tom, Dick and the Devil who happens to call."

"Hope that's not meant to include me?"

"Of course not." She had suddenly remembered that her peace and comfort depended in a large degree on the attitude of the police. "We know you've come to tell us all about this horrible murder in the subway."

"Sorry to disappoint you, but I know very little more than the papers have already printed. My errand's quite a different one, I want another look at your vanished maid's trunk."

"Very well, I'll have the new maid pull it out for you, or no, I'll go along myself."

They had already left the room when Fisk remembered something and stepped back to the open door.

"I've phoned headquarters that I can be reached here for the next half hour—expecting certain important information that may come in at any moment—please call me if I'm wanted on the phone."

Shirley stayed with him while he again went over the rather scanty contents of the missing maid's trunk, so that for the first time Dr. Munro found an opportunity to really talk to Fay; an opportunity of which he made such good use that she was delicately flushed and starry eyed when the half-expected call for Inspector Fisk came in.

"That you, Inspector?" operative Nelson's voice came over the wire.

"Yes, Inspector Fisk speaking."

"Good. Think I've learned the Subway Girl's identity. Can you meet me at the morgue? I'm bringing along another model to make sure."

"Right, I'll be there."

He put down the instrument and started for the door, hesitated a second, then addressed Dr. Munro. "I seem to be acquiring the habit of asking you to come along, doctor, this is the second time I've done it. But I know you're interested and it's not a bad idea to let you look at the Subway Girl—they think they've found out who she is."

"'Interested' is a mild way of describing it—I'm eaten alive by curiosity!" After the briefest of farewells the two men left Shirley Tabour and her cousin to their own devices, then chartered a taxi whose driver was shaken from his normally blasé outlook on life by Fisk's snapped direction. "The morgue."

"I expect you think my attitude more or less that of a prying old woman." Dr. Munro laughed half apologetically as their taxi threaded a slow way through the congestion of Park Avenue. "But the fact is, the science of crime detection has always fascinated me. I'm an omnivorous reader on the subject and have formed a sort of theory which I've never before had a chance to test."

"If I remember rightly you once before mentioned a pet theory; why not let me hear it?"

"Oh, it's a simple enough thing. It so happens that I've done a good deal of big-game hunting, as well as watched several much more expert sportsmen trailing elusive or dangerous beasts. It's occurred to me to wonder if the basis underlying man-hunting isn't much the same."

"As how, for example?" Fisk sounded no more than tepidly interested.

"Well, don't both require infinite patience, infinite attention to insignificant details of landscape and spoor? In the one, every hoof or paw print, every particle of browsed-on verdure, or torn kill, is carefully studied—the hunter tries to read from them, what the animal he's after has done, and intends doing; in the other, fingerprints take the place of claw marks; disturbed furniture, dropped ashes, used weapons, the place of chewed grass and slain prey,—the man-hunter tries to make them tell his criminal's type and what he's likely to do next. Is the idea far-fetched, or is there a certain similarity?"

"There may be a likeness,—though it never struck me before,—particularly in the personal qualities needed by hunters of beasts or men. We might try working it out together, but no, I've a friend, a playwright named Sydney Traherne who dabbles in criminology as a sort of pastime—I'd better take you to see him some evening and let you measure your theories against his."

Munro seemed to cordially welcome the idea and they discussed it, but had arrived at no settling of a definite time for the meeting when the morgue was reached.

They found Nelson waiting, a tall slender girl dressed in the extreme of the latest fashion, in tow.

"This is Miss Mildred Daily, inspector, she's a model at Emory Shale's wholesale dress house and from my description of the Subway Girl she's pretty certain it's Nora Munday; one of their models who didn't show up for work to-day."

"Bring her inside and we'll make sure."

After one glance at the body pitilessly displayed on its marble slab, Mildred Daily shrank back with a repudiating cry.

"No, oh, no! That's not Nora!"

But the inspector had experience of how violent death and the dread atmosphere of the morgue can so change a scrap of human flotsam that it often escapes recognition by those nearest and dearest to it in life; he firmly insisted that Mildred take a second, more deliberate look.

"You're right. I guess it's her," was the model's revised verdict. "If somebody'll give me a whale-of-a-hooker I'll give the poor kid another look and make dead sure."

The desired stimulant being promptly supplied and even more promptly consumed, Mildred studied the "Subway Girl" as she had come to be called during the hours when her identity remained a mystery.

"Not a doubt it's Nora"—her voice held unquestioning conviction—"but she sure is changed something awful. Nice guy that was, that took her for a ride."

"Meaning literally, or in the sense the phrase has lately acquired?" Inspector Fisk instantly wanted to know.

"I was remembering what she told me yesterday afternoon about the date she had," Mildred explained, adding reproachfully: "Say, do we have to stay here while you drag out everything I ever knew about the kid?"

Thus adjured, Fisk borrowed the office of his friend Jim, wherein the somewhat shaken Mildred was supplied with another drink and a much-needed cigarette.

"Now let's get down to business." Fisk settled, note book in hand. "First of all, what was the girl's full name?"

"Nora Munday." She added an address on the lower west side.

"Any relations that we ought to notify? By the way, it's odd they haven't reported her as missing."

The Perfumed Death 53

"Couldn't. She'd nobody but a bedridden father— God knows what'll become of him now, Nora's gone."

"There was absolutely no other relation?"

"None, living or dead, that either Nora or the old man ever spoke of. I've been down to their dump a good few times and got the notion he'd seen better days and wasn't wanting any truck with people who knew him then."

"Happen to know the father's name?"

"Yes, it's Howard Munday. He got smashed up in some kind of an accident before I knew 'em at all and Nora's been supporting him ever since. Tough on the kid, I'll say."

"How long have you known the Mundays?"

"Going on a year, maybe a bit more."

"Know if she'd a sweetheart?"

"Not what you'd call a regular one. Nora didn't play round much, hadn't the time, or money to buy the right clothes."

"Don't models draw fairly decent salaries?"

"Sure, providing they work steady, but not the kind that runs to invalid fathers *and* evening duds."

"Now, getting down to what Nora Munday told you yesterday afternoon, exactly what was it?"

"Well,"—Mildred had so far recovered her normal poise as to sit upright in the stiff-backed chair and carefully preen herself. Evidently, in spite of the somewhat gruesome circumstances, she was beginning to enjoy being the center of so much masculine attention—"the kid blew in yesterday morning a bit late but chipper as a lark, and while we changed into working slips, told me how a swell guy in a peach of a car damned near ran over her on the way home Monday night. Guess it was a close call, because the guy stopped and apologized, they got to talking and even if it was chancy, Nora let him drive her home. Seems he fell hard and wanted to make a date, which same was done for last night."

"She didn't tell you his name?"

"Now, I ask you, do men running big Packard cars chase round handing out visiting cards to us working girls? Course Nora didn't know his name, not his real one anyhow."

"How do you know he drove a Packard car?" Fisk sharply demanded.

"Saw it waiting when we quit work. I didn't get a look at the guy's face 'cause he was on the off side and as soon as Nora opened the door and hopped in beside him, he let her hum."

"I suppose you didn't glance at the license number?"

"Why would I? There was no knowing it meant turning into a murder car."

"Hardly that. The girl was found on a subway train, you know."

"Mere detail." Mildred's shoulders mounted in a shrug she fondly imagined distinctly French. "It was in the car she was done in, wasn't it? Must have been trouble, mustn't there? otherwise what'd Nora be doing riding a subway train when she started out in the Packard?"

"You'd better give us a description of the car."

"Big, dark gray, seven passenger, that's all I had time to see."

A few more questions and Inspector Fisk let Mildred go. He planned an immediate visit to the Subway Girl's bed-ridden father, and for the third time invited Dr. Munro, whose absorbed interest he found stimulating, to "Come along."

6

The landlady of the dismal boarding house, the address of which had been supplied by Mildred Daily, regarded Inspector Fisk and the doctor with a suspiciously wary eye. While not suspecting them of a connection with the police force, whom she associated only with blue uniforms and brass buttons, they were obviously of a class unfamiliar to her ken.

"Yes, I've a father and daughter here, name of Munday," she cautiously admitted when questioned.

"The daughter's missing, isn't she?"

"Well—" The landlady's mind could be almost seen scurrying about in search of the safest answer. "Well—it's not time for Nora to be home from work."

"And she wasn't home at all last night, was she?"

"Can't see as what my boarders does is any of your business."

"Come, come, my good woman," the inspector's voice was suddenly crisply authoritative, "you'd best stop hedging. We're from police headquarters and the girl, Nora Munday, was murdered last night."

Under which piece of information the landlady's guarded defiance evaporated, leaving her a collapsed bundle of tears and woeful plaints touching the havoc such scandalous notoriety would bring to her supremely respectable house. She was barely able to sob out directions how to reach the top floor domicile occupied by the Mundays.

It was a big, low ceilinged, down-at-heel room into which they entered in response to a muffled, "Come in," though some attempts had been made to brighten it by the addition of rather flaring cretonne curtains at the single dormer window, and a cover to match spread over the one comfortable article of furniture the place boasted; a wide, brass posted bed, on which lay the room's prisoner.

Howard Munday was a man well over sixty, Leonine-headed and evidently naturally tall for the long lines of his body could be seen stretched, pathetically immobile, under the gaudy bed cover. As the two strangers entered he struggled up onto one elbow, staring at them out of bloodshot tormented eyes.

"Nora! Has anything happened to my baby?"

It was one of the moments when Conway Fisk actively loathed his profession, but there was no evading the necessity of breaking the black news, and he did it with a tact and a gentleness that would have astonished those knowing him only in his respect of merciless pursuer and no less merciless judge.

It was half an hour before the old man, who at first only piteously begged to be left alone with his grief, was able to answer the inspector's necessary questions, then he realistically described the horror of his long wait for Nora.

"Though I prayed God it wasn't true, I knew she was dead," he ended; "otherwise she'd never have left me so long without word."

"She was a devoted daughter, then?"

"The best, most unselfish feminine creature that ever trod the earth!" her father solemnly declared.

"Now, returning to strictly mundane matters—have you had any food or attendance to-day?" Fisk insisted on knowing.

"Oh, my wreck of a body's been taken care of." The invalid waved a vague hand toward the disordered tray on a decrepit bureau. "There's a sewing woman in the house whom Nora paid to look after me. It was my mind—the awful fear of what'd happened, that nearly drove me insane."

"It seems a shame to ask so many prying questions, Mr. Munday, but we've got to find the brute who killed her and there's no way of telling exactly what information may help. Had your daughter any sweetheart, any one sentimentally interested in her?"

"I think not. She sometimes went to supper or a picture show with different young men living here in the house, but there was nothing serious, nothing that could in any way account for—what's happened."

"I suppose no one benefits at all by her death?"

"Benefits? How could they, we'd neither of us any money of course."

"Nor insurance made out in somebody's favor?"

"Our pocket book, or rather Nora's, since I've been incapable of earning anything for the past four years and before that had lost my entire fortune, didn't run to the taking out of insurance policies."

"Apparently we must look elsewhere for the motive," the inspector decided as he and Dr. Munro finally took their leave. He had not told the old man of Nora's venturesome ride with the unknown owner of a gray Packard, and on the way out cautioned both the subdued landlady and the sewing woman against letting him see the newspaper accounts of the murder. "No use torturing him more than necessary. He seems the sort to be heartbroken over the girl's risky adventure even apart from its dire results, so why shatter his ideal of her complete perfection?"

"I'm afraid I was thinking more of what's to become of him, physically," Dr. Munro acknowledged. "That landlady doesn't look as if she possessed an ounce of charity, she'll probably pitch the old man out on the street if his rent isn't forthcoming."

"Oh, that side will be taken care of," the inspector absently assured him. "But was there ever such an apparently motiveless crime? And it's hard to believe the unknown who took her for a ride actually killed her, when it would have been so much easier and less risky to simply leave her somewhere on the road—supposing, of course, she refused to pay the expected price for her evening's entertainment."

"Could it have been purely an accident?"

"I'd be almost tempted to believe it if it wasn't for the similarity between her death and Cyril Kenwick's; but—two people dying with that strange perfume in their mouths and a rubber band wrapped round their third fingers? No, deliberate murder's the only possible answer, though I don't mind admitting I've never before been quite so completely at sea to the when and how, let alone the who."

That evening Inspector Fisk again sought counsel of the still maddeningly indifferent Sydney Traherne.

"My dear Fisk, won't you try to understand that New York crime waves don't, at the moment, interest me in the least?" he besought, comfortably a-lounge in the depths of his favorite chair. "My comedy's coming along nicely and until it's finished, or the creative wheels stick and refuse to go around, your talk of weird scents and motiveless murders leaves me absolutely cold."

"You're a heartless, self-centered brute," the inspector grumpily informed him. "Aren't you going to so much as offer an opinion?"

"How the deuce can I obligingly offer something I haven't got?" Traherne patiently inquired. "Only an idiot acquires an opinion without at least superficially considering the facts—and I haven't done even that."

"Then you ought to be properly ashamed of yourself! Here two innocent young lives have been ruthlessly snuffed out and you haven't the decency to be faintly interested!"

"After all, old dear, it's your job, not mine," Traherne pointed out, his oddly striped eyes in which tiny spokes of alternate black and gray radiated, spoke-wise, from the pupil, meditatively watching the flight of expertly blown smoke rings mounting ceilingward.

"Nobody pays *me* to dash round chasing elusive criminals. And as for 'innocent young lives,' according to your own story this Kenwick youth was a bit of a rotter, while you know next to nothing about the girl and, in passing, I might remark that thoroughly right-minded young females don't go joy-riding with total strangers."

"It doesn't seem to have been a habit, in fact I rather think it was the first time Nora Munday ever did such a thing."

"Pity it proved so emphatically the one time too many."

"Oh, you're hopeless! I might as well go off and grouse by myself."

There was a discouraged note in Fisk's voice that touched his friend's very real affection, though it left his indifference to the case itself quite undisturbed. More with the idea of cheering Fisk than of offering any real help, he suggested:

"Why don't you concentrate on finding somebody who knew both victims and had more or less of a place in their lives?"

"Because there isn't anybody—not a single person knew both young Kenwick and Nora Munday. They moved in totally different worlds with, so far as I can discover, not the shadow of a connecting link between the two."

"Some young bloods *do* go in for models, you know, though I'll admit the betting average's higher on chorines."

"You're the second person who's hinted at that possibility—the other was Shirley Tabour—but we haven't been able to find anything to prove that Cyril Kenwick ever saw the girl much less knew her. Besides, she was evidently a confiding kid, witness how she told Mildred Daily all about the proposed joy-ride. I doubt her keeping a romance of the type you and Mrs. Tabour suggest a complete secret."

"Still, there must be some connection, unless you're willing to attribute the elastic rings and scented lips to pure chance; all you have to do is systematically dig for it."

"As if half the homicide bureau hadn't been spading away for dear life," the inspector snorted his contempt of the other's aloof detachment, "unearthing for their pains, exactly nothing!"

"So?" Traherne seemed to be at last fixing at least a part of his attention on the inspector's baffling problem. "At what station was it you said Nora Munday got on the subway train?"

"Van Cortlandt Park, if the word of the one passenger who noticed her can be trusted."

"Why not try to learn if any gray Packard car stopped for repairs at a garage in that vicinity late Tuesday night?"

"You think they may have had a breakdown?"

"Exactly. That would account for the Munday girl's going home alone in the subway while the man, whoever he was, waited for the trouble with the car to be fixed up."

"Wouldn't she have waited with him?"

"Not if the job promised to take some time. She'd be too anxious to get home, as you say she wasn't in the habit of staying out late."

"At least it's an idea," the inspector conceded. "I'll put some of my men to work on it first thing in the morning, or no, I'll phone and have them start inquiries to-night."

"For the Lord's sake don't be so impetuous," Traherne begged. "Cultivate the meditative calm recommended by that most excellent teacher of moderation, Gautama Buddha."

"Oh, hang your heathen gods! You always trot them out when you want to be particularly aggravating. Why shouldn't I start hunting that possible breakdown as quickly as possible?"

"No earthly reason except that we haven't thoroughly discussed the subject—for instance, did you happen to notice if the girl's slippers showed signs of a long walk?"

"Meaning that if they did she'd probably been dropped by the wayside and obliged to walk to the nearest station?"

"Not only that, the Packard may have broken down some distance from the subway, or Grand Central lines, say somewhere in the Riverdale section."

"As it happens Nora's shoes were flimsy, stilt-heeled things—God knows how women manage to even toddle in such footgear—and they were as fresh and undefiled by roadside dust as the proverbial lily of the field."

"Then that settles it, go ahead and set your bloodhounds on the trail of an ailing Packard."

While the inspector went to use the telephone in the foyer Sydney Traherne changed his smoking jacket for an ordinary coat and collected hat and gloves.

"Yes, we're going out"—he nodded in answer to Fisk's inquiring look. "Your disposition's badly frazzled and your brain full of cobwebs—for both of which ailments I prescribe a ride on the top of an uptown bus. Nothing like it for giving one a feeling of calm superiority over the helpless little roadsters and things, wildly honking their woes on the pavement so far beneath one."

The spring evening was crisp, but not cold enough to make riding in the open air unpleasant and as their bus crawled along Fifth avenue, threaded a tedious way across 57th and up to 72nd, finally reaching the open stretches of Riverside Drive, Inspector Fisk felt his overtaut nerves slowly relaxing.

"Not a bad prescription of yours, Sid, one does get a bit smothered seeing only skyscrapers and the crowded pavements and the old Hudson gives one a wholesome sense of the unimportance of puny human affairs. What say we get off and walk for a while?"

They left the bus at 84th street and were crossing the sidewalk toward the strip of park running near the river when Inspector Fisk caught sight of a small approaching figure.

"Hold on a second, there's Zoe Panza. I wonder what the dickens she's doing way up here?"

The girl had seen them, or rather Conway Fisk, almost at the instant when he spied her and came toward them with her usual air of lighthearted impudence.

"Lady-hunting by any chance? Or is it safe to stop and say howdy?"

"After that remark you'll jolly well come along and smoke a cigarette with us," the inspector informed her, "otherwise you'd spread lurid tales of a police official and noted playwright gone on the loose on Riverside Drive. Oh, you two haven't met, by the way." He introduced them and all three cut down into the park, following one of its winding paths until they found a bench to their liking.

"Any use asking if you're up here in quest of fresh air or a fresh scandal?" Fisk inquired as he held a light for Miss Panza's cigarette.

"Not a particle. I never tell anybody exactly why I'm anywhere."

"Shows a nice trusting disposition."

"Doesn't it? Also saves a tremendous amount of brain fag and keeps me a halfway truthful person; think of the lies I'd have to invent if I once started explaining my movements to every chance acquaintance. If you've ever noticed, people more or less respect a tall woman's privacy, but when a girl's as small as I am they're generally possessed by a tiresome longing to watch over and protect her."

"Regardless of size, I've never met a woman who struck me as more thoroughly capable of paddling her own canoe. Why do you know," the inspector turned to more directly include his friend in their conversation, "two years ago no one in the newspaper game had ever heard of Zoe Panza, now she's one of the best-known reporters in the city and she accomplished it on her own, as far as I've been able to discover, with nary the trace of a pull."

Even by the uncertain light of a neighboring arc lamp Traherne could see how the girl's dark little face flushed under the inspector's praise, though she countered it with a gently amused chuckle.

"Well, aren't we small-sized people usually credited with more than our due share of interest in other people's business? And after all a well-developed bump of curiosity, helped along by a keen scent for news, are the things most needed by a reporter. How's your Perfumed Death Case coming along, by the way?"

"Little wretch, christening it by that lurid title," Fisk reproached her. "And as to coming along, it's doing nothing of the kind, thank you, I'm up against a blank wall."

"Too bad," her sympathy was apparently genuine. "Can't the doctors decide what killed the two victims?"

"You're enough on the inside to know they can't agree. Some of them insist the poison was injected into the blood, and the rest swear it must have been taken internally because they can't find the least sign of a skin puncture."

"Which opinion are you favoring?"

"I scarcely know. So far they've been unable to find any traces of poison in the stomach contents but on the other hand there's a chance they may have failed to get a reaction because they're applying the wrong tests; every last one of them admits they can't pin a name to the poison used."

"How about Shirley Tabour's missing maid? Found any trace of her?"

"Nary a one. She seems to have melted into the earth. Of course her going off like that is devilishly suspicious."

"Does rather suggest that she knew something about young Kenwick's death, doesn't it?"

"Yes, and she was one of the several people who washed up dishes, or in her case glasses, Cyril used that last day of his life."

They continued to discuss the case for some half hour or more then Zoe, after a glance at her wrist watch, declared she must go. They walked back to the drive where Zoe boarded an uptown bus which Traherne watched with a certain meditative interest as it rolled away toward Grant's Tomb.

"Rather an attractive scrap of femininity," he observed while they stood waiting for a bus to take them in the opposite direction. "Is she always as gayly lighthearted as to-night?"

"Always. She flashes in and out of newspaper row like an irresponsible little sunbeam. I never remember seeing her without at least the echo of a laugh or a smile, though as to what she's like in strictly private life I haven't the remotest idea—she never admits any one into the sanctum of her home, or even tells where it is."

7

The following morning, when a beautifully appointed limousine drew up at her door, Howard Munday's landlady decided that there were compensations for being so closely connected with a murder case; her sudden association with the wealthy classes lent her a reflected glory that must, she felt, greatly enhance her popularity in the neighborhood.

"Yes, m'am, this is the house, m'am," she assured Fay Redmond who had stepped from the limousine and rather doubtfully ascended the shabby front steps. "I'll take you up to Mr. Munday's room myself."

On the way Fay slipped a little roll of bills into the woman's grubby hand.

"Please see that he has every possible comfort. I'd rather give it to you than offer it to him personally—and—I'll bring or send some more before that's exhausted."

"I'm sure the Lord'll bless your kind heart, m'am, helping the poor stricken father—and what name did you say, m'am?"

"I didn't say." Fay's brown eyes could be very frigid when she chose. "Please ask Mr. Munday if he cares to see me."

The bed-ridden man was only too glad of a visitor from the outside world, any one who might even momentarily lighten his burden of bleak despair. Fay told him how she had read of his daughter's tragic death and felt impelled to at least offer her sympathy, though she refrained from mentioning any more substantial expression of her pity.

They were on the road to becoming quite good friends when another visitor, Dr. Munro, arrived. Under the circumstances it was natural enough when they both left Howard Munday's sick room, for Fay to suggest driving the doctor wherever he wanted to go. Then, on the way uptown, he begged that if she had no other engagement she would take pity on a poor lonely bachelor and lunch with him.

"I'm afraid you're judging me by my cousin"—Fay's tone held gentle but unmistakable reproof—"and really I'm quite a conventional sort of person."

"Pardon, if my longing to know you better outbalanced my discretion." His expressive eyes told of such frank admiration that Fay felt her resolution weakening and womanlike, promptly retired behind further barriers of explanation.

"Most people follow the modern trend toward informality but my husband happens to be terribly old-fashioned; he dislikes having me lunch or dine alone, even with men whom I've known for years."

"That must make life rather dull for you, particularly as Mrs. Tabour mentioned his being away a great deal. But perhaps you love him enough to gladly accept such restriction." It was voiced more as a statement than a question and Fay discreetly ignored it, changing the subject to Howard Munday whose forlorn situation seemed to have touched the depths of her pity.

The personal note was not struck again until they reached the apartment house where Shirley Tabour lived, then Fay realized that after offering to drive him wherever he liked she had neglected asking his destination.

"I'm so very sorry, perhaps you wanted to be left somewhere downtown?"

"No. In fact seeing Howard Munday was my only errand; I wanted to cast a professional eye over his physical condition and at the same time leave some money with his landlady."

"We were moved by the same impulse." She smiled at him, adding: "If you're going nowhere in particular, perhaps you'd like coming up to see my cousin?"

"If that includes seeing you as well, I most certainly should."

"Of course. I intend lunching with her as my husband is busy to-day."

In the end Dr. Munro lunched with both ladies and Shirley Tabour, much to her own surprise, found herself occupying a distinctly secondary place—the handsome doctor making no real effort to veil his preference for Fay.

"Well, it's about time Fay had a little fun," Shirley silently told herself. "God knows how she ever stands that husband of hers, and the fact that he's madly in love with her must make it all the worse." After which reflection she retired still further into the background, watching Fay's half thrilled, half shy acceptance of the doctor's evident interest with friendly, it might almost be said, approving eyes.

Later, on that same afternoon, Shirley's ex-husband, Jerome Tabour, received an anything but pleasant shock when Inspector Fisk's professional card was brought into his private office. For a long moment his heavy-lidded eyes stared at the inoffensive bit of cardboard that yet carried such possible threat of dire unpleasantness, then he glanced at the curiously watching secretary.

"Say what he wanted?"

"No, sir."

"Probably something about the murder case my charming ex. is mixed up with," Tabour hopefully decided. "Might as well bring him in and get it over with."

When admitted to the private office Inspector Fisk at first left the object of his visit undeclared; he was mentally gaging his hand and deciding on the most effective method of attack. Such leisurely procedure further jangled Jerome Tabour's already irritated nerves so that he presently blurted out a direct question.

"What was it you wanted to see me about, Inspector? I'm taking it for granted your call wasn't prompted by a desire to talk politics and the weather." Then, as his visitor delayed answering while he lighted a cigarette, Tabour's impatience drove him on. "Something touching my ex-wife's connection with this Kenwick murder case, perhaps?"

"No, not that case, another one," Conway Fisk answered with a maddening deliberation, still apparently more interested in the proper drawing of his cigarette than in their conversation. "You own a seven passenger Packard car, I think."

The pen with which Tabour's fat white fingers had been nervously playing, dropped on the desk with a small sharp clatter but his answering voice sounded almost unconcerned; the realization of his worst fears had in a large measure restored his shaken self-control.

"Yes, a gray one, 1930 model."

"You drove it last Wednesday night?" Tabour nodded and the inspector went pitilessly on. "Taking it from the garage a little after four on Wednesday afternoon you dismissed your chauffeur, telling him he wouldn't be wanted at all that evening, then you drove down to 27th street and collected a passenger, namely, little Nora Munday. After that I admit ignorance of your movements until you entered a garage in the neighborhood of Van Cortlandt Park at about 11:30—you were alone at the time and merely stated that your car had broken down a few blocks away, giving its description, license number, and keys to the man in charge of repairs, who promised to immediately have car towed in, whereupon you left the garage, remaining away for the better part of an hour and returning with what the repair man classed as 'One hell of a grouch.' By that time the trouble with your battery had been adjusted and you were able to drive off under your own power. Is my synopsis correct?"

"Perfectly, and I suppose what you want is a filling in of the lapses?"

"Exactly."

"You're aware that the Munday girl wasn't a friend of mine? That I'd never seen her, in fact, until the previous night?"

"So I understand."

"Am I permitted to ask where you got your information?"

"As regards the shortness of your acquaintance or your movements on Wednesday?"

"Both."

"Nora Munday told another model of her dinner appointment, and the same girl saw Nora enter your car when they both left the wholesale dress house where they worked. This other model, a girl named Mildred Daily, was also able to supply a description of your Packard so when we started inquiries at the garages near the station where Nora Munday was known to have boarded the subway train, we had little difficulty in tracing it; though, of course, the fact that you'd had a breakdown was pure assumption on our part."

"If I'd realized the likelihood of your making it I should have come forward of my own accord," Jerome Tabour admitted.

"It might have been wiser," was the inspector's dry comment. "The fact that you didn't suggests you had something to hide."

"My God! You don't think *I* killed her?"

"So far I've stated no opinion either way. You'd better give me your version of what actually happened night before last."

"You've heard how I almost ran over Nora Munday, and the close call led to our fixing up the Wednesday night date?"

"Yes, she also confided that episode to her friend Mildred."

"Fond of advertising, wasn't she? If the little fool had kept her mouth shut I'd have been spared a lot of notoriety."

"Under the given circumstances most men would consider themselves lucky if they escaped with no worse," Fisk rather grimly informed him.

"Is that a threat?"

"Hardly. Rather a suggestion that so far you've a good deal to be thankful for. Mind getting on with your story?"

"Well, I met the kid outside the building where she worked as per arrangement. We drove out the Albany Post Road to a quiet little place near Tarrytown where we dined and had a few drinks. To be quite honest, Nora Munday didn't quite come up to expectations; I'd been rather caught by her air of fresh innocence but it proved a bit insipid at close quarters. I didn't much care when she insisted on starting back home at an unearthly early hour. I drove back through Yonkers and meant striking Riverside Drive, but as you know my battery caused trouble and finally went dead not far from Van Cortlandt Park. When I went in the garage to see about having it fixed up I left Nora close by, meaning to charter a taxi for the rest of the trip—the little prude sneaked off before I came out and I couldn't find her, must have got scared that I wouldn't take her safely home to her precious father as per request."

"You were hunting for her during the time your car was under repair?"

"Yes, though you're wrong in saying I was away from the garage nearly an hour, it wasn't anything like so long. The trouble was I'd imbibed a good few drinks and wasn't too sure on exactly which corner I'd left the girl parked, so wandered round the neighborhood looking for her. It wasn't till afterward I caught the idea that she'd probably scuttled up to the elevated station—the subway trains run above ground at that point, as of course you know—then I went back, found my car ready for use and drove on home."

"That completes your story?"

"I imagine so. You can see for yourself the Munday girl was nothing to me, I'd no earthly reason for wanting to kill her."

"It's only because of the apparent lack of motive that I'm not taking your connection with the case more seriously," the inspector unfeelingly assured him. "You may not have quite realized that your direct connection with the second poison victim, and the more remote one through your ex-wife with the first, when taken together, place you in a pretty ticklish situation."

"But—good God, man, I never so much as saw Cyril Kenwick!"

"So you say. Still, your ex-wife was engaged to marry him, there might be a jealousy motive there."

"It's rank absurdity; when I divorced Shirley I was thundering glad to be rid of her!"

The inspector's shrewd blue eyes studied him with a cool detachment. "As I said before, it's lack of plausible motive that has so far kept suspicion from actually settling on you. But God help you if a convincing motive does crop up in either case! Now, getting back to business; were you and Nora Munday alone all evening?"

"If you mean alone except for the other diners, yes."

"Was she out of your sight at any time?"

"Only when she went to the ladies' dressing-room before we had dinner, and, come to think of it, again just before we left the road house."

"Did she mention meeting any one she knew during either of the two visits?"

"No."

"They were both brief?"

"And otherwise she was under your eyes the entire time?"

"Yes."

"Are you inclined to be observant?"

"About average, I should say. Why?"

"Wondering if you noticed anything physically wrong with the girl; if she seemed unduly tired, feverish, ill in any way."

Jerome Tabour gave the suggestion a moment or two's careful thought. "Can't say I noticed anything wrong with her—she only seemed more or less scared."

"Possibly your attentions were a little over-heated."

"Oh, well, if a fool girl doesn't expect to be made love to she shouldn't go joy-riding with strangers." Tabour's tone was distinctly aggrieved. "Most of them haven't such sparkling intellects that a man cares to dine and wine them for no return but the pleasure of their conversation."

"Well," much to Jerome Tabour's relief the inspector showed signs of departure, "I think that about finishes my list of questions. There's just one piece of advice I'd like to offer—if you want to avoid serious trouble, don't leave town until after the double inquest that's being held to-morrow."

8

"Twelve-thirty! I'd no idea it was so late." Inspector Fisk made a tentative movement preparatory to dragging his long body from the depths of one of Sydney Traherne's great leather chairs.

"No special hurry, we've neither of us a wife to complain if we sit up late. Have another peg." His host poured some of the velvet-smooth old brandy, added a generous dash of soda, and handed the glass across the table between them, remarking: "You're no more ready for bed than I am—climax of the second act, which refuses to behave properly driving sleep from my eyes—mystery of the second poison murder doing the same for yours."

They sipped their drinks in companionable silence, Fisk presently complaining:

"I really did expect something to turn up at to-day's inquest—but it left us exactly as much in the dark as we were before! Hang it all, let's talk about something else!"

"As for instance? You know nothing but your 'Perfumed Death' case really interests you. Terrible, to be such a creature of one idea!"

Before Fisk could frame a fitting retort they were startled by the sharp whir of a distant bell on which some one seemed to have placed a finger and forgotten to remove it.

"Sounds like somebody in the deuce of a hurry—" Fisk cocked a quizzical eye at his friend. "Expecting a, ahem, visitor, by any chance?"

"No. It's probably a mistake in the bells, our front hall isn't too well lighted."

Traherne went to investigate, reappearing a few minutes later with Zoe Panza surprisingly in tow.

"Now, what on earth—?" The inspector jumped up, eying her incredulously.

"Didn't know our friendship had ripened so fast, inspector dear?" Zoe greeted him with an infectious little chuckle. "Don't look so astonished—this is really my first visit and it's you I'm looking for."

"Mean to say you pursue the elusive news item all night as well as all day?"

"Not quite that bad; at present I'm on the track of something extra special and need help."

"Oh, I didn't flatter myself you'd hunted me down for the pleasure of my company," Fisk retorted. "Time to tell us about it comfortably, or must we rush off somewhere?"

"Plenty of time," she assured him after a glance at the clock. "Whatever happens isn't scheduled to begin until between two and three." She proceeded to make herself thoroughly comfortable, accepting a modified edition of the brandy and soda the two men were drinking, and lighting one of her own cigarettes. "You both know that most reporters who at all specialize on criminal news have their own pet stool-pigeons," she commenced. "Mine's a nice sleek little gambler who's been ever so useful in the way of passing on inside information concerning various crimes and criminals—for a due consideration, of course. Well, about two weeks ago 'Slithers,' that's my little pet's fancy name, gave me a tip that a certain high-stepper of the underworld had his eye on a gentleman who owns an immensely valuable collection of jewels. He couldn't say precisely what was being planned but knew there was something in the wind, and promised to notify me if he heard further details. It seemed a tip worth following, so I kept a motherly eye on said jewel collector until your Kenwick case broke and rather switched me off his track. Then, last Thursday afternoon, Slithers phoned me he had more news. I met him and he told me the designs on the jewel collection were coming to a head. Hilary Thorp's the jewel owner's name, by the way, either of you happen to know it?"

The name was unfamiliar to Sydney Traherne but Inspector Fisk instantly recognized it.

"Isn't he the eccentric old recluse living somewhere in the middle seventies just off the drive? Man who's supposed to possess more unset stones than exist in any other one place in America outside of a museum?"

"That's the party, and of course you've guessed I was working Slithers' tip when I ran into you two night before last." Zoe reached for a second cigarette before going on. "It seems the cracksman, whose name I'm not yet ready to divulge, had planted a girl of his in the Thorp house as a maid; she passed him plans of the interior, necessary key patterns and so forth, then quit her job before the actual trouble started because she's known to the police. I told you Slithers is a sleek, smooth-mannered little brute; he'd been getting round the girl by making love to her and she'd spilled that much, but didn't know herself exactly when the robbery was to be pulled. I sent him back with instructions to stick close to the girl, letting me know any further developments, then, reasoning that as the Thorps were suddenly short a maid I might be able to land the job, I fixed up to look the part—you know the type, nice, meek, school-girly little thing—and applied for it, saying the girl who left was my cousin and had been taken suddenly ill while visiting my home; she hoped the housekeeper would let me fill her place until she was better."

Zoe suddenly stopped, to fling an impishly gleeful grin at the intently listening inspector.

"I've a taking way with the women, whatever you men think of me; the dear old soul fell for me at sight and told me to settle in then and there. Later in the evening I asked permission to go out and telephone my family as the Thorp servants aren't allowed to use the one in the house. I was headed back to the new job when I ran into you."

"So that's why you weren't overly pleased to see us," Traherne remarked as she paused to finish the remainder of her brandy and soda.

"You noticed that?"

"Yes. I saw you a second before Fisk did, and caught that your first impulse was to dodge—also, though I said nothing about it to him, I watched the uptown bus you boarded and saw you get off at the first stop; from which fact I naturally concluded that your real destination was somewhere below 84th street and you'd started the other way with deliberate intent to deceive."

"Well, I wasn't ready to talk then," Zoe shamelessly explained. "If I'd mentioned a threat to Hilary Thorp's jewels the police would have made some move likely to scare off my cracksman."

"And of course you'd sooner have the robbery actually take place so you could get a scoop for your rag of a paper, than warn us in time to prevent a daring crime!" the inspector wrathfully accused.

"Of course, I'm a reporter, not a detective," Zoe retorted, quite unabashed. "Now, if you'll stop finding fault with my behavior and let me go on with the story, I'll carry on from Thursday night. Yesterday and to-day nothing happened; I got away long enough to attend the inquest but otherwise have been sticking close to the job. Then, about nine this evening, I saw Slithers parked on the steps of an empty house just across from the Thorps. His being there told me he'd important news for we'd arranged his only showing up like that as a last resort—you see, I wasn't allowed to receive phone calls any more than to send them.

"Having been out once to-day I didn't dare ask leave again, so signaled Slithers I'd join him as soon as I could make it and settled down to wait until the house-keeper went to bed. She didn't, as it turned out, for presently a fake telegram arrived calling her to the bedside of a dying sister. Naturally the poor dear didn't know it was faked and scuttled off in such a mad rush she neglected telling either Mr. Thorp or his man, Duncan, that she was going.

"Next came a phone call for the old man's nephew, Teddy Thorp, saying his best pal was in trouble with the police somewhere on Long Island—I couldn't catch the exact spot—and begging him to come to the rescue. Of course that was also a frame-up designed to get him off the premises, which it did in short order; he streaked off like greased lightning.

"That left only four of us in the house, the old man Thorp, who's as weak as a cat, his confidential man, Duncan, another maid servant and myself. I got her off to bed and then joined Slithers, who told me the robbery's planned for to-night, as was pretty obvious once people began being called suddenly off the scene."

"To-night!" Fisk was on his feet, already starting for the door. "Why didn't you tell us sooner?"

"Patience, old dear, there's plenty of time, things aren't due to commence until somewhere between two and three and it's not quite half past one."

"Why the devil didn't you report to headquarters instead of hunting for me? Protecting the Thorp house isn't up to my department anyway."

"No. That's why I cut the time so close you'd have to take on the job rather than waste any getting in touch with the proper department," Zoe cheerfully informed him. "I like working with you so much better than with any other inspector."

"And of course your personal preference is all that matters! But you're right, the time's too short to waste any of it. I'll phone and have a squad from the nearest station house meet me at the Thorps."

"No." Zoe again detained him as he made for the door. "They'd get there in time to warn off the thief. Have them gather in the next street, on foot, then you can post men so as to trap the cracksman once he's entered the Thorp house."

"Right. I'll use your phone, Traherne."

"Are you coming along?" Zoe glanced at her host as the inspector hurried out into the foyer. He hesitated a second, then nodded.

"I've tried to keep my nose out of police matters lately—but to-night my car can get Fisk up to the Thorp house quicker than a taxi and besides I feel you need looking after—"

"Seem sure I mean tagging along."

"So sure that I'm not even trying to cut you loose—it would be sheer waste of valuable time. Come on, Fisk must be nearly through phoning and luckily my car's parked outside."

On the way uptown they frankly ignored lights and speed limits, Inspector Fisk explaining to any officers who attempted interference that they were on police business of the utmost urgency.

When the cross street behind the Thorp house was reached Fisk directed his friend to draw up at the curb. The street seemed deserted but once they were out of the car uniformed figures began appearing from various lurking places for the phone call had told them what to expect. Before assigning the men to their posts Fisk turned sharply to Zoe Panza.

"Is your pet stool-pigeon watching the house?"

"Yes."

"Go meet him then, and if he reports no one's gone inside, slip in yourself. Can you manage it?"

"I purposely left the basement door on the latch."

"Good. Then if you're not back in five minutes Traherne and I'll approach the house singly, from opposite ends of the block—be ready to let us in. In case your man reports the thief already at work, come back here and we'll rush the place. Got that?"

Zoe merely nodded, then slipped away with a noiseless speed that made Traherne look after her, an odd glint in his eyes. She found Slithers waiting in the appointed areaway, exchanged a few hurried words with him, then crept, cat-footed, to the basement door. It was still unlatched and she pushed it open, waiting with the door slightly ajar for Fisk and Traherne.

In spite of her cool courage the girl was breathing a little rapidly as first one tall figure, then the other, neared the Thorp house and joined her in the darkened basement.

"Your man reports the coast still clear?" Fisk whispered, his lips almost against her ear.

"Yes, but he says the plan to keep Teddy Thorp out of the way must have miscarried; he came back only a short time after I left."

For a time there was absolute silence in the pitch-dark entry; only the muffled honk of a belated car came from the street outside and none of the three moved or spoke. Then the inspector discarded inaction, fearing the thief for whom they watched might effect an entrance through the front door, which was beyond their present range of vision.

"Sydney, I'd like you to stay here with Miss Panza while I go up to the main floor." He still spoke in the softest of muted tones. "It's already well after two. I'm beginning to fear young Thorp's unexpected return has scared him off."

He melted away into the darkness, leaving the other two tensely on watch. Followed another period of complete silence, which to Zoe's strained nerves seemed hours long, then it was pierced by a smothered explanation and the sudden flash of an electric torch.

"Come here!" the inspector's sibilant whisper reached them from the head of the basement stairs.

Guided by his flashlight they tiptoed to where he bent over a figure stretched full length on the floor of the main hall, close to the head of the basement stairs.

"I tripped over him while making for the front door," Fisk explained. "Looks as if there'd been a slip somewhere—we're too late!"

"It's Teddy Thorp." Zoe had taken the shock with a quietness that astonished both men when they later on had time to remember it. "He's been chloroformed, hasn't he?"

"And effectually tied up and gagged." Fisk was digging for his police whistle. "I'll call in the men from outside—if the thief's still in the house we'll catch him. Plenty of light and noise are our best bets now."

"You'll terrify old Mr. Thorp," Zoe warned. "Can't we rouse the others without bringing the police in just yet?"

"Too chancy—our man might get away while we were gently waking the household. Also, judging by the sample we've found, they're probably all safely trussed up."

Disregarding her further protests he found his way to the front door, opened it, and blew two quick blasts. The men who answered were hastily told of the finding of young Thorp, bound and chloroformed, then set to search the lower floor and basement while Fisk, Traherne, and two picked men mounted to the floor above; Zoe, whom they were all too busy to stop, unobtrusively trailing after them.

In the upper hallway the men first entered two empty bedrooms, the doors of which stood wide open, then halted before a closed door that resisted their tentative efforts to open it.

"That's Mr. Thorp's room," Zoe volunteered.

"Better break in the door," Fisk decided when repeated knockings brought no response.

The two regular police officers set their shoulders against the wood, which creaked protestingly, finally splintering inward so they could force a way into the stifling darkness of a room which fairly reeked of chloroform. Fisk's first move was to fling open a couple of windows, his second to find the electric switch and flood the place with light; in the bed lay an old man sunk fathoms deep in a drugged slumber.

"At least he's not dead." The inspector's tone told how much he had feared for the aged jewel collector's life. "One of you men go hunt up the nearest doctor—there's probably one in the neighborhood and at this hour it'll be quicker than phoning to drag some medico out of his bed. Hark! What's that?"

A muffled pounding came from some distant part of the house; a rhythmic beating quite different from such sounds as drifted up from the searchers on the floor below. Zoe's small figure flitted out to the hall and she was halfway up the stairs leading to the next floor before Inspector Fisk stopped her.

"Where the devil do you think you're going?"

"That must be the maid I told you about. She's the only one sleeping up there to-night."

On investigation they found the girl locked in her own room, quite unhurt but frantically terrified. As she was the only conscious person they had so far discovered, Inspector Fisk instantly pounced on the weeping girl.

"Tell us what happened? Did you see the man who broke in? Were there more than one? How'd you come to be locked in your own room?"

"Honest, I don't know no more than a new-born babe," she sobbingly assured him. "After Mabel here"—with a vague gesture toward Zoe Panza—"and I came up to bed I didn't see nothing, or hear nothing, till just a little while back when I woke up real sudden and caught kind of funny noises coming from downstairs. Then, when my door wouldn't open so I could find out what was happening, I got that scared I thumped on it to make somebody hear and let me out."

The inspector might have persisted in trying to extract some scrap of helpful information had not Zoe just then plucked at his sleeve, drawing him a little to one side.

"What's become of Duncan?" she whispered. "Surely, if he's not drugged like the rest all this noise would have waked him, and—he sleeps in the room where the jewels are kept."

"Where's that?"

She led the way down to the second floor, and reentered Hilary Thorp's bedroom where the old man still lay, breathing stertorously, while Sydney Traherne and one of the police officers worked over him.

"It's an extension built out at the back—the only way of getting in is through this room."

"But there's no door," Fisk objected, eying the rear wall of the big, old-fashioned room rather blankly.

It was not for nothing that Zoe had lived in the house for even so short a time; she unhesitatingly crossed to a big tapestry and pulling it aside showed him a door set in flush with the wall but otherwise perfectly normal looking. It readily yielded to Zoe's hand but when she reached for the light switch just inside it refused to work.

"Something gone wrong with the lights, you'll have to use your flash."

As she had said, the jewel room was a fairly large extension added on at the back of the original building. One wall, the one separating it from Hilary Thorp's bedroom, showed a line of small safes sunk into the plaster at about breast height, each with a single large letter painted under it: D. R. E.—the initial letters of various precious stones. As the inspector's flashlight played over the round metal doors they could see that all of them were more or less ajar.

"Holy mackerel! He's made some clean-up!" Fisk groaned. "Why the Blue Hades didn't you pass on the tip in time to prevent this?"

"Sorry," she absentmindedly apologized, her eyes vainly struggling to pierce the darkness. "I wonder what's become of Duncan?"

"He's Hilary Thorp's confidential man?"

"Yes. A sort of cross between a secretary and a valet. He's immensely strong and always sleeps in here to guard the collection."

Rapidly the little ray from Fisk's torch picked out one article of furniture after another, finally settling on a wide couch made up as a bed, its disordered state showing that though now empty, it had been slept in.

"He's not here. Perhaps he was in with the thief and went off with him."

"No." Zoe's small head shook a definite refusal to doubt Duncan's entire honesty. "He must be somewhere in the house. We've got to find him!"

She was right; under her insistence the inspector's flash explored the room, foot by foot, presently lighting on a limp, muscular looking hand that lay, palm up, close to the edge of a long library table; behind it Duncan lay stretched, the open glassily staring eyes and features convulsed into a mask of mortal agony, telling them that he was already dead.

The inspector dropped to his knees, then suddenly leaned closer, an ashen pallor overspreading his face:

"Christ! It's the Perfumed Death again!"

9

Because of the absence of proper light by which to examine it, the jewel room was locked and a man stationed at its solitary door to prevent any one entering or leaving until the coming of daylight permitted an effective search.

No trace of the thief could be discovered anywhere else in the house, and it seemed evident that he had left before their arrival, despite Slithers' report that no one except Teddy Thorp had entered, and no one at all left the house after Zoe Panza's departure.

"Think he's playing crooked, or did he take a nap?" Fisk asked, but the girl refused an opinion, beyond saying that the little gambler had hitherto always been straight with her. "Well, it can't be an inside job since every one's either locked up, chloroformed, or dead—and you say the house hasn't a rear exit. Your stool-pigeon must have either sold you out or gone to sleep, there's no other explanation possible."

"Oh, have it your own way, inspector dear." Zoe's hands went out in a quick little gesture that disclaimed either opinion or responsibility. "I'm going down to see if they've brought in a doctor."

She found him in one of the lower rooms, valiantly struggling to bring Teddy Thorp back to consciousness. Relieved of his bonds and the stifling gag, Teddy lay so white and limp that Zoe was aware of a sudden stab of dread.

"Is he going to die?" she found herself asking.

The strange doctor who had been called in from a neighboring apartment house favored her with a slightly contemptuous glance.

"Certainly not. It takes more than a few sniffs of chloroform to kill a youth of his physique. In fact, he's likely to wake up very soon now; you might give directions to have some strong coffee made, and then sit with him while I go upstairs and attend to his uncle."

As a result it was on Zoe Panza that Teddy's opening eyes first lighted. He stared at her dazedly for a second or two, then grinned with a rather dismal attempt at cheeriness.

"Hello, Beautiful—mind telling me what the hell's happened to my head—*and* my tummy?"

"You've been drugged, that's all. Keep quiet and I'll give you some black coffee."

"Hold on." His brain was beginning to clear a little. "What's it all mean, and why are you wearing outdoor clothes in the middle of the night?"

"Don't talk yet, and as for my clothes, I'm a newspaper reporter who got a tip that some crooks had designs on your uncle's jewels and took on the job of housemaid with the idea of catching them."

"Successful?"

"Lord, no! They've made off with every last jewel."

"It'll about kill the old man," Teddy gloomily prophesied. "That collection is emphatically the one thing on earth he cares about. Why, a tidal wave or some little thing like that could wipe New York off the map and Uncle Hilary not turn a hair, so long as he was able to save his precious collection."

"Maybe at least part of it can be recovered, but at present it's a missing quantity."

"Does he know?"

"I think not, last I heard he was still unconscious—chloroformed just as you were."

"Not quite the same," Inspector Fisk spoke from the doorway behind them. "The officers who unbound this young gentleman and carried him in here, tell me they found a sponge and empty chloroform bottle lying close to his head; also that while his ankles were tied tightly enough, the rope round his wrists seems to have been mainly designed as decoration—it allowed free play of both hands."

"Who the devil are you and what are you driving at?" Teddy resentfully inquired, as the inspector and Sydney Traherne came fully into the room, closing the door behind them.

"Nothing—yet." Fisk stood regarding the prostrate youth with a none too friendly eye. "We'd like your version of what happened to-night, if you're enough recovered to give it."

"Are you also newspaper men, friends of Mabel's?"

"Mabel was only a name assumed for the housemaid part," Fisk coldly informed him. "The lady is Zoe Panza, a well-known reporter who, this time, has succeeded in making the devil's own hash of things. As for me, I'm an inspector from police headquarters and this is Sydney Traherne, a friend of mine. After which explanation perhaps you'll condescend to tell us about to-night."

"See here, my good man—" Teddy was angrily beginning, when Zoe's small fingers administered a warning pinch.

"Better do as he asks."

Instantly Fisk's irritation flashed out at her. "I'll thank you to keep out of this, young woman; God knows you've already caused enough trouble."

"That's right, blame me because our friend the cracksman switched his time schedule!"

"That reminds me; down at Traherne's you refused to give his name, but you'll have to pass it on now—we've got to try and catch him before he has time to leave the state."

Zoe considered, then decided on parting with the desired name. "It was Gentsy Judd; of course you know him."

"As it happens I've never met the gentleman, but I've heard of him; he's fairly well known. I'll go phone headquarters that he's wanted."

While he was gone Zoe poured a cup of strong coffee for Teddy, who was recovering from the effects of the chloroform with a rapidity only made possible by youth and extreme good health. When she found he was able to sit up and drink it unassisted she offered Traherne some coffee and also helped herself. On his reentry Fisk's mood seemed slightly more cheerful; perhaps sending out the drag-net for Gentsy Judd made him feel that matters were at least started in the right direction.

"Now, young man." He drew a chair close to Teddy's couch and settled down, notebook in hand. "They've smashed the light connection in your uncle's jewel room so we can't properly examine it to-night and the old man himself is still unconscious, therefore the best we can do at the moment is get your version of events. First of all, Miss Panza tells me you're Hilary Thorp's nephew and only living relative; is that accurate?"

"Quite."

"You've lived with him some years?"

"Ever since my parents died when I was still in my early teens."

"You're the old gentleman's heir?"

"Why do you ask that? His life's in no danger, is it?"

"Not according to the doctor. Still, one likes being posted on matters touching inheritance. You haven't yet answered my question."

"I can't."

"Can't, or won't?"

"Simply can't. I've no idea how uncle Hilary means leaving his jewels, whether to me or to some museum—and I understand he's very little else to leave."

"Meaning that their loss will seriously cripple him financially?"

"More or less wipe him out, I imagine. Of course he owns this house, though I shouldn't be surprised to find it's heavily mortgaged, and I suppose he's some money in the bank, but Miss Panza here, while she's only been in the house a couple of days, can tell you it isn't run on a line to fit its exterior. Ever since I can remember my uncle's skimped on everything, except his beloved jewels. Food, heat, clothes, everything's cut down to the lowest possible minimum so he can swell his collection by buying an occasional ruby, diamond, or other stone. A few times illness or some other sudden emergency has forced him into selling a jewel or two, and I give you my word the necessity nearly broke his heart; he was miserable for weeks afterwards."

"Queer passion, sacrificing everything else to his mania for precious stones. He makes nothing out of the collecting game, then?"

"Heavens no! As I tell you he never sells a jewel if he can possibly hang on to it. He must have started out with a pretty big fortune, practically all of which he's tied up in his hobby."

"So you don't know if you're his heir." The inspector dropped the collection in favor of more personal matters. "Do you and your uncle get on well?"

"So-so. Now and again he hears I'm in debt and we have a set to—otherwise things run pretty smooth."

"Does he pay said debts, outside of your regular allowance?"

"You've got me all wrong, inspector." For the first time Teddy's engaging grin lighted a face that, while not handsome, was very likable. "I'm no pampered son of wealth. Ever since I left high school—my education didn't run to college—I've earned my own living and paid Uncle Hilary for my board. When I fail to make both ends meet and run into debt, why it's just too bad—the old man leaves me to square things up the best way I can."

"And you have some particularly pressing debts at the moment?"

"Not more so than usual; I'm chronically getting dunned by one creditor or another. It's only when they apply to Uncle Hilary instead of to me that fireworks start."

"Anything of the sort happened just recently?"

"No. We've been living in peace and harmony for a couple of months back."

"Now, we'd like hearing how you spent to-day, or rather yesterday, for we're well into Sunday morning."

"Let's see—it was a half holiday at the office; we close Saturdays at one o'clock. I lunched down town with two other clerks and then went to a picture show."

"With them?"

"No, alone."

"See any one you knew?"

"Not that I remember."

"H-m-m, well, it's of no consequence, alibis don't mean a damned thing in this case." Which remark, though it had a somewhat cryptic sound to Teddy, the others knew referred to his ignorance of how long the unidentified poison took to operate and therefore how many hours before death it would need to be administered. "You came home at what time?"

"Around six, or a little later."

"And dined alone with your uncle?"

"Yes."

"Did he seem in his usual health and spirits?"

"As far as I remember, yes."

"And Duncan; how about him?"

"Duncan? Why, where does he come in?"

"We'll take that up later. At present I'd like an answer to my question."

"Duncan's a morose, close-mouthed sort, not given to airing his troubles. I happen to know he's recently been suffering from indigestion but he said nothing about it last night."

"Do you know if he was out at all yesterday?"

"He was. In fact, he came up the basement stairs wearing his hat and topcoat as I let myself in the front door."

"You didn't mention his going out." The inspector turned a reproachful eye on Zoe.

"Didn't I? Well, I couldn't remember to tell you everything, and I'd no earthly reason to think it mattered."

"You knew it, then?"

"Surely. There was no secret about Duncan's having the afternoon off."

"We left you dining with your uncle, Mr. Thorp; what happened afterwards?"

"Nothing in particular." Teddy was glancing from one to the other, plainly puzzled by the inspector's sudden brief interest in Duncan. "We played a few games of double Canfield and then my uncle went upstairs. I stayed downstairs reading until a phone message came in, supposedly from a pal who was in trouble over the speed laws and wanted me to drive down to Long Island and help him out of a scrape. I started off in perfectly good faith but crossing the Queensboro bridge overtook the car of another friend who lives in Jackson Heights—thinking he might care to tag along I stopped to tell him about Roberts' hurry-call-for-help and learned he'd just left Roberts, who was peacefully calling on his best girl and in no scrape whatever. Naturally I thought somebody'd been trying to spoof me, so turned around and headed for home."

"You can give us this second man's name and address so we can have him verify the meeting on the bridge?"

"Surely." Teddy unhesitatingly supplied it.

"Now, go on."

"Leaving my car at the garage I walked the two blocks from there to the house, let myself into a pitch-dark hall, and instantly met my Waterloo."

"You were attacked the moment you entered the house?"

"The moment I closed the front door and reached for the light switch."

"It was too dark to see your assailant?"

"Much. Also he gave me no chance to be inquisitive—before it dawned on me there was anything wrong somebody with a good working knowledge of ju-jitsu laid me out cold and pretty—I don't even remember the chloroform or being tied up."

"At least you know if there was more than one man?"

"Sorry, I can't even swear to that. As I tell you, I'd no time for observation."

"Humph, if you ask me, the story sounds just a little thin. One would suppose that, finding yourself called off on a wild-goose chase like that would make you suspicious enough to enter the house with reasonable caution."

"But, suffering snakes, I hadn't the ghost of an idea it meant anything more serious than a practical joke! Some moron trying to be funny. And see here, inspector, I've answered all your questions with the patience of a woolly lamb—don't you think it's about time you let me ask a few?"

"Depends on what they are."

"First off, I'd like knowing how Miss Panza learned somebody had designs on Uncle Hilary's collection."

"No harm telling you that, her paper will enlighten you if I don't. It seems she's been cultivating a pet stool-pigeon named Slithers, and it was he who gave her the tip."

"But why didn't she pass it on to the police so the house could be guarded, instead of coming here herself, disguised as a maid?"

"Ha! That's a question any sane human not bitten with the reporting bug would be likely to ask." Fisk emitted a small snort of wrathful disgust. "You probably aren't acquainted with the true news-hunter breed; to them nothing on God's green earth really matters when compared to a possible scoop for their own particular scandal-sheet. Miss Panza was afraid if she told us what was in the wind we might make some move that would scare off the thief and cheat her out of a sensational robbery."

"That's not fair, inspector dear," Zoe mildly cut in. "You know I planned getting you here in time to catch Gentsy Judd red handed. It wasn't my fault if he set forward his time of operation."

"At the incidental cost of a human life!"

"What's that? Mean to say they've killed Uncle Hilary?" Teddy had risen, to start rather unsteadily toward the door. The inspector gently pushed him back on the couch.

"Duncan—not your uncle."

"He's actually dead?"

"Yes. We found him upstairs in the jewel room." Fisk's voice held increasing gravity. "So far he's been left exactly as we found him—I told you the thief put the lamps in that room out of commission—we haven't even let a doctor examine him because it's vitally important that nothing in that room should be disturbed until there's light enough to make sure we overlook no clews."

"Poor old Duncan!" The boy seemed rather dazed by the disastrous news. "Was he killed because he tried to defend my uncle's jewels?"

"His being their guardian was the reason for his removal, of course, but he wasn't given a chance to actively defend them. You've doubtless read some newspaper accounts of this unknown poison that's claimed two previous victims—leaving them with mouth and lips saturated with a strange flowery fragrance? Well, Duncan appears to have met an exactly similar fate."

"I know, this young Cyril Kenwick and the little dress model, Nora Munday—" Teddy broke in excitedly. "I've read about them. But I thought nothing was stolen in either case. Weren't they crimes of a different order than plain robbery?"

"We thought so," Fisk admitted, then checked further confidences as he remembered Teddy might be classed as a possible, though improbable, suspect. "Now, you've talked enough, young man; better go upstairs and rest. You'll need all your strength later in the day."

"The beastly stuff has left me a bit wobbly—I wonder if Miss Panza would help me up to my room?"

"Of course." Little Zoe seemed to find nothing absurd in the idea of her arm being required as a crutch by a youth easily three times her size, but the two older men exchanged amused glances.

Traherne waited until the door closed behind Zoe and her self-elected charge, then quietly crossed to a far corner of the room and stooping, picked up a small cardboard square.

"What's that?" Fisk's eyes had intently followed the movement.

"A nicely engraved visiting card—name of Mrs. Joel Redmond."

"Redmond? Redmond?" For a second the name failed to convey any message to the inspector's considerably befogged brain, then he swore softly. "By all that's holy that's Fay Raymond—the charming Shirley's cousin! Does it mean that we've at last found a link?"

"Hard telling. Why not have in the genuine maid and see if she's enough recovered from her fright to tell us where the card came from?"

"Perhaps Zoe knows."

"If she did she'd surely have mentioned it, the name of Fay Redmond is as familiar to her as to you. I think the housemaid's the one to question."

On inquiry they found the girl was down in the kitchen, whither she had repaired to be near some of the policemen on duty in the basement, as she was afraid to stay alone in the upper regions. When questioned about the calling card she was able to give a quite clear description of the visitor who had left it.

"Very pretty she was, and dressed something beautiful, all in a goldish kind of brown color as just matched her eyes and hair."

Conway Fisk had happened to see Fay wearing the costume described, which fact helped to banish his last shred of doubt.

"Sounds like Fay Redmond, all right," he told Traherne, who had never seen her; then to the girl: "When did this lady call?"

"This afternoon, I mean yesterday afternoon, sir," she stumblingly explained. "It do get a person that mixed, being woke up so in the very middle of the night."

"Do you know if she'd ever been here before?"

"I don't think so, sir, I'm most sure she was a stranger."

"Who did she ask for?"

"Mr. Hilary Thorp, and I asked was it important because he don't much like seeing people. She said it was and—I hope you won't think me prying, sir, but when he come downstairs I couldn't help hearing her say she'd a ruby she wanted to sell."

"Yes? This is getting damned interesting! Do you know if Mr. Thorp bought it?"

"Yes, I do, sir, for when he rung for me to show her out I heard the lady thank him kindly for buying it."

"Good girl! You've a pair of ears well worth owning!" If she had belonged to his own sex Fisk would undoubtedly have slapped her on the back, as it was he administered a fatherly pat on the nearest plump shoulder. "Now run along to the kitchen and see if you can't scare us up a bite of breakfast, one of my men will be glad to help, I'm sure." He was almost chuckling with suppressed satisfaction. "What say, Sydney? When things have a bit straightened out here shall we pay the lovely Fay a visit and ask about this ruby she sold the old man?"

10

As soon as the day had fairly dawned Fisk and Traherne locked themselves in Hilary Thorp's jewel room and commenced an intensive search—leaving orders with the man on guard outside that they were on no account to be disturbed until the medical examiner arrived.

Taking due precautions against destroying telltale fingerprints which must be preserved for the expert's camera, they went over the entire room inch by inch, Traherne finding what appeared to be the most valuable and at the same time the most puzzling clew so far discovered.

From the narrow space left between the end of an upright bookcase and the wall, he unearthed an oval case about two inches long made of the finest basketwork, so closely woven that it resembled the straw of a panama hat except that instead of being white, or cream colored, various shades of blue, green and orange were blent in a slightly garish pattern: but what fascinated both men was the fact that, though empty, the little case smelt of the same exotic perfume that clung to Duncan's dead lips.

"May I take it home to examine at leisure?" Traherne stood with the case extended on his open palm.

"You mean you're coming in with me?" his friend demanded.

"I seem to have no choice. Three murders inside a week are going a little too strong—you need all the help you can get."

"Right. Take the case and we'll say nothing about it at present. It'll probably confide more secrets to you than it would to one of our best experts."

They discovered no other clew that seemed important and entertained very scant hope that any of the finger marks decorating the row of looted safes would prove to be those of the thief. By the time the medical examiner, police photographer and fingerprint expert arrived they had about concluded their search, so left the new comers in possession while Inspector Fisk went to question old Hilary Thorp, who had been moved to another bedroom to avoid the constant disturbance caused by people passing in and out of the rifled jewel room.

Lacking his nephew's splendid health the old gentleman was making a much less rapid recovery, being still quite unable to leave his bed or even attempt sitting up. Still, he managed to give the inspector a coherent account of what little he knew.

At some time during the night, he had no way of determining the exact hour, he had suddenly wakened with the sensation of another presence in his room. Foolishly calling out a question, instead of remaining perfectly silent, he had been instantly attacked by the unseen intruder whose strong fingers closed on his throat, choking him into silence and eventual unconsciousness—from which he had only roused to find himself surrounded by doctors and police officers.

When told that his nephew had met with almost similar treatment he evinced no concern whatever, but news of the successful robbery reduced him to a pitiable state, made vocal in frantic appeals and lavish offers of reward for the recovery of his adored collection.

Zoe Panza had long since departed, bent on furnishing her paper with an eye-witness' account of the night's events, and the housekeeper presently returned from the wilds of Jersey, whither she had been enticed to the home of a particularly robust sister. She was unable to offer any helpful evidence and insisted she had seen no suspicious looking characters of either sex recently lurking near the Thorp house.

At about ten o'clock Inspector Fisk entered the drawing room where Traherne had waited during his rather prolonged session at the phone.

"Sorry, Syd, but I'm afraid you'll have to take up the Fay Redmond angle alone. There're a thousand and one things I ought to do; chiefly try getting on the track of Gentsy Judd, of whom my men can't find a trace."

"Shall I be able to reach the lady? I've never met her, you know."

"Oh, my card will get you in, say I sent you—anyway she'll probably talk more freely to you alone than she would if we went together. Afterward give me a ring either here, or at headquarters."

It was a very agitated young woman who presently received Traherne in the stately drawing room of the Redmonds' east side home. She had so far succeeded in keeping her association with the now famous poisoning cases from her husband, but the invasion of her home by a man bearing Inspector Fisk's card bred a fear that she was about to be drawn into such close contact with the investigation that further secrecy would become impossible.

The first few minutes of their interview were spent by Traherne in trying to allay her fears. It was not until she had lost a good part of her nervousness that he broached the subject of her yesterday's visit to Hilary Thorp.

"My call has no connection with your cousin," he told her in answer to a question from her. "Nor even with the Kenwick murder case."

"What, then?" Fay's golden-brown eyes flickered hurriedly from his face to the open door behind him.

"Shall I close it?"

"Please." Then, when the shut door secured them a greater degree of privacy, she anxiously demanded the reason for his visit.

"Inspector Fisk wants you to tell me anything you know about Hilary Thorp."

"Why, I scarcely know anything at all!" She was either genuinely astonished or a superb actress. "Except, of course, that he's quite a famous collector of jewels."

"We're aware that you possess that much knowledge—also that you visited him yesterday afternoon."

"Oh, dear! I didn't realize the police were watching me so closely!" She had suddenly flushed a vivid scarlet and Traherne gathered an impression that the blush had nothing whatever to do with her recent visit to Hilary Thorp.

"If you *will* leave personal cards about—" He smiled at her, a confidence-inspiring friendliness in his oddly striped eyes.

"I don't understand why you're so interested in that queer old man."

"Because his house was robbed last night. The entire jewel collection is missing, including, I suppose, the ruby which you sold to him."

"Did he tell you about that?"

"I came to ask questions rather than answer them. The inspector would very much like to know why, with a husband as wealthy as yours, you needed to sell a ruby to Hilary Thorp."

"For the same reason that people generally dispose of their jewelry—I wanted some ready money."

"Why not apply to your husband?"

"It was for a very special purpose; one that he doesn't approve."

"Surely one that you can confide to Inspector Fisk, through me."

"No." Fay's tone held a very definite refusal. "And now I'm going to ask you to please go. There's really nothing I can tell you about Mr. Thorp, I never saw him until yesterday, and I'm afraid my husband may come in at any moment. Oh." Her breath caught with a sharp little gasp. "It's already too late! How can I ever explain you?"

He had barely time to answer: "Simply follow my lead," before the door opened and the owner of the voice both had heard outside entered the room.

Joel Redmond was at least twenty years older than his wife, probably more, yet so well preserved and perfectly groomed that one gained an impression of ripened maturity rather than age. He would have been handsome had not the clearly chiseled features been marred, almost distorted, by a sardonic sneer, evidently chronic, to judge by the deep lines it had etched. Only for an instant, as his full dark eyes lighted upon Fay, a strange flicker of tenderness softened his entire face, then vanished as his gaze traveled on to Traherne.

"Do I intrude?" From his lips the question sounded very like a sneer.

"Quite the opposite." Traherne turned to him with the air of one seeking a possible ally. "Perhaps you'll help me persuade Mrs. Redmond to alter her decision. I've been trying to interest her in our wonderful new accident policies and she can't seem to realize their immense superiority over those offered by any other insurance company."

"No?" The suspicious dark eyes flashed from one to the other, then settled on Traherne's intelligent, but quite unimpressive face, apparently deciding that he was not a type to be feared where women were concerned. "Sorry to disappoint you, but I think we already carry all the insurance necessary. Therefore we need waste no more of your valuable time."

He sauntered across to open the door through which Traherne passed to the keeping of a hovering footman with a relief unguessed by the master of the house.

"No wonder Fay's afraid of him," he reflected, on his way to the nearest drugstore and telephone booth. "Must be an extremely disagreeable person when he's really roused and what a nice hole I should have been in if he'd shown an interest in my insurance company and asked for some of its literature. Nevertheless the man's much more deeply in love with his wife than many a more amiable husband. Wonder if that fact simplifies or complicates life for her?"

Calling first the Thorp house and second police headquarters, he made an appointment with Conway Fisk for later in the day, then went home for a much-needed meal and freshening up; it had been an undeniably hectic twelve hours into which Zoe Panza and her stool-pigeon's tip had so unexpectedly pitchforked both men.

As Traherne neared headquarters on the way to keep his appointment with Fisk, he was surprised at sight of Zoe Panza and young Teddy Thorp seated in a roadster drawn against the curb; both of them so absorbed in conversation that they failed to notice his approach.

It was his first sight of Zoe by daylight and some vaguely exotic quality about the girl which had previously puzzled him, seemed much more pronounced. He was unable to determine exactly where this suggestion of the unusual lay; whether in feature, voice or manner; it was more a subtle impression than a tangible difference from the majority of well-groomed girls of her age. A something disquieting and yet attractive. Then she turned and saw him, whereupon the puzzling quality vanished behind her sunny smile.

"You see I've enlisted another aid," she called to him. "Mr. Thorp is bent on helping me trail the fugitive news item; though, just between ourselves, I believe that's only an excuse, what he's really after is the recovery of the stolen jewels."

Traherne felt inclined to agree with her about the newsquest being no more than an excuse, but remembering the boy's rapt absorption in her small dusky face before his own coming had disturbed them, rather doubted the accuracy of her guess at Teddy's real motive. After inquiring about his uncle and congratulating young Thorp on the rapidity of his own recovery from the effects of the chloroform, Traherne left them and entered headquarters, where he was almost immediately admitted to Inspector Fisk's office.

Dr. Munro was already there. He had telephoned after reading the newspaper account of the third mysterious poisoning, begging to be allowed at least a passive share in an investigation which was rapidly acquiring nation-wide fame.

"Just because I was the first person to call Inspector Fisk's attention to this novel, sweet-scented death, I insist on making myself a nuisance by feeling a sort of proprietary interest in the whole case," the doctor half apologetically explained to Traherne when the inspector had introduced the two men. "I expect he wishes I'd stop encroaching on his professional activities and stick to my own."

"On the contrary, intelligent interest always helps," Fisk asserted. "Sydney here, is a bit too detached to form a really satisfactory audience. Also he's devilishly inclined to sit hard on my pet theories." Then, settling down to business, he asked what Traherne had learned from Fay Redmond.

"Practically nothing. She acknowledges selling a ruby to Hilary Thorp yesterday, but refuses to say why she needed the money beyond stating that it was for some purpose of which her husband disapproved. Then he came in and not wanting to get the lady into trouble I discreetly faded out."

"It's just possible I can suggest a reason for Mrs. Redmond's sale of the stone," Dr. Munro unexpectedly put in. "I happen to know, quite by accident, that she's paying Howard Munday's expenses."

"What's that?" The inspector favored him with a frankly incredulous stare. "Why as far as I know Fay Redmond never saw the second poison victim's father, much less paid for his keep."

"You're quite mistaken. I met her at Munday's boarding place the morning after you and I first went there, and I know she's been to see him at least once since then."

"She's an old friend?"

"I think not. In fact Mrs. Redmond told me her pity was stirred by reading of his sad situation and she went to offer help just as any other charitably inclined woman might do."

"Have you any reason to think her husband disapproved?"

"Yes. Later I heard Fay tell Shirley Tabour that he had forbidden her going near Munday."

"In face of which, you think she's still visiting him?"

"I met her leaving the boarding house only yesterday morning, and the sewing woman who nurses Munday told me how generous the brown-eyed lady had been; they apparently none of them know her name, so of course I didn't enlighten them."

"You realize what this means, Traherne?" The inspector turned to his friend, a gleam of something very like excitement in his usually quiet eyes. "We've at last found some one connected, however remotely, with all three poison victims!"

"Inspector!" Dr. Munro emitted a horrified gasp. "You're not dreaming—" He broke off, unable to properly frame his question.

"That Fay Redmond is a triple murderess?" The inspector entertained no such scruples. "Perhaps not quite that bad, but at least she's the only person we've so far discovered who knew all three victims."

"But she didn't!" Munro heatedly contradicted. "She knew nothing of the Mundays until after Nora's death—and from what you yourself tell me of her visit to Hilary Thorp there's nothing to show she even saw this man Duncan."

"Nevertheless Fay's the one and only person known to have come in contact with all three groups," Fisk stubbornly pointed out. "Remember she was in her cousin's apartment while Cyril Kenwick was there on the last night of his life; she claims not to have seen him, but it's possible that she had an opportunity to tamper with the cocktail shaker or the glasses—all of which were carefully washed up by the maid who afterward vanished.

"Next we find her visiting Nora Munday's father the very day after the subway-girl's identity became known—there's a chance that the money supposedly donated from motives of pure charity is actually hush-money paid to keep Howard Munday from telling of a friendship between Fay and his daughter. While her visit to Hilary Thorp, ostensibly for the purpose of selling him a ruby, at least took her inside the house on the very day it was robbed and we've no means of knowing precisely who she saw, or did not see, during her visit."

"Of all the absurd, far-fetched rigmaroles I ever heard that line-up of facts distorted out of all plausible shape is the worst!" The doctor sounded thoroughly incensed. "What equally ridiculous motive have you imagined?"

"Oh, I'm not actually accusing her at this stage," the inspector answered quite unresentfully. "Only calling your attention to possibilities that have got to be followed up."

"Then you don't purpose instantly arresting Mrs. Redmond?"

"No need of sarcasm." The inspector seemed disinclined to take the doctor's anger at all seriously. "She's not the only one whom it's possible to regard with a certain amount of suspicion; there's Teddy Thorp for example."

"But the papers say he was found trussed up and insensible."

"Without adding that a sponge and empty chloroform bottle were found close to his head, or that the rope tying his hands left them free play so he might easily have drugged himself. Facts which I believe Zoe Panza suppressed more through consideration for Teddy than because I asked her to. Mind you, I'm not definitely stating that the boy robbed his uncle, still it's curious that the stool-pigeon saw no one else enter or leave the Thorp house after Zoe had left him to watch it."

"He still sticks to that story?" The question was Traherne's.

"Can't be shaken, and denies having closed his eyes or left the areaway during the whole time Zoe was gone."

"How about this cracksman who Slithers says intended stealing the jewels?"

"Can't be found, though I've had experienced men combing his usual haunts since dawn. Also we've rounded up dozens of stool-pigeons for questioning but not one of them admits seeing Gentsy Judd for days past."

"Nothing turned up at pawn shops or fences?"

"No, though it's a trifle early to hope for results at either. The thief won't attempt unloading any jewels while the hunt's in full cry."

"And I suppose the fingerprint experts found nothing of consequence?"

"Not a strange print anywhere in the suspected rooms; in fact the only ones left in the jewel room itself belonged

THE PERFUMED DEATH   107

to Hilary Thorp, Duncan, or Zoe Panza—it seems she dusted the room both Friday and Saturday."

"One thing's been especially puzzling me." Traherne, producing pipe and tobacco-pouch, thoughtfully commenced preparing his favorite smoke. "Why was the key to Hilary Thorp's room removed from its lock? There was nobody in the house able to go to the old gentleman's assistance in case he roused and called for help; in fact, why lock the door at all?"

"Probably only a precaution against his waking and telephoning in an alarm; there's no telephone in his bedroom. As for the key's removal, it wasn't carried far, one of my men found it in the lower hall."

Dr. Munro, who had been quietly listening to their fire of question and answer, here put in one of his own.

"If Teddy Thorp's at all involved in the robbery he must have an accomplice; otherwise the stones would still be hidden somewhere in the house. Why didn't this stool-pigeon see the accomplice leave?"

"I'm beginning to believe that Slithers sold out to the other side and is lying about nobody going in or out," the inspector declared, "but so far we can't prove it. Oh, by the bye," turning toward Traherne, "did the little wicker case betray any secrets?"

"So far I've not had time to examine it." Traherne paused to apply a second match to his pipe, which declined to light properly, then added: "It's safely stowed away in my laboratory and to-morrow I'll give it a careful going over."

"Is Zoe Panza herself absolutely to be trusted?" The doctor had apparently been following some private train of thought.

Before Fisk could answer his question the office door opened without the ceremony of a knock and two dancing black eyes peered round its edge.

"Did I hear somebody taking my name in vain?"

"Come on in," the inspector invited. "The rest of you might as well follow your ears. This is Dr. Munro, and what he was saying about you is none of your business."

Zoe promptly availed herself of the permission to join their conference. "I've come to ask a favor, inspector dear."

"Pretty courageous considering the hash you made of things last night."

"Why persist in blaming me if people say they intend doing a thing between two and three when they really mean a couple of hours earlier? What I want, now, is a card or note to Fay Redmond."

"Why?"

"Well, you know the old adage, 'Set a thief to catch a thief,'—not that we're either of us anything less than models of the strictest virtue, but you know we women can penetrate further under a lovely feminine surface than you men; we're less dazzled by the glamour. Who knows, perhaps I'll be able to tell you secrets about the beauteous Fay that you'd never discover unassisted."

11

"I may be altogether wrong, but at present I think Fay Redmond's connection with the various poison victims purely accidental—the mystery goes deeper than we've so far guessed."

Zoe and Dr. Munro had both gone, leaving the two friends alone in Conway Fisk's office which, by now, was blue with the breath of pipe and cigar.

"You may be right." The inspector's tone betrayed discouragement. "Frankly, I've no fixed opinion of my own. I don't know what to think. It's a case where all three of our usual cornerstones are missing. We've found no adequate motive for any of the murders—we don't know how long the poison takes to act so can't eliminate anybody by means of an alibi—and so far we've no really plausible suspect to concentrate on."

"Then you admit Fay's simply the best you have to offer; and not too convincing at that?"

"At least she's better than the rest. A fanatically religious father who may, just conceivably, have considered himself the Lord's chosen instrument to end the error of Cyril Kenwick's ways; an ordinary, middle-aged joy-rider who, if he killed Nora Munday must have done it only because she resented being made love to; and, worst of the lot, industrious, likable Teddy Thorp who could easily have picked his chance and stolen the whole collection without killing its guardian or raising such a general hullabaloo."

"Where does Gentsy Judd come in?"

"I'm not sure that he *does;* hang it all, I'm not sure of anything! It's the most senseless, topsy-turvy case I've ever encountered. Why, we don't even know what poison was used or how it was administered!"

He lapsed into discouraged silence, eyes moodily watching the smoke rings ascending from his cigar. For five minutes or more neither man spoke, then Traherne knocked the dottle from his pipe and straightened from his lounging pose.

"Somewhere there's an overlooked clew pointing to a connection between the poison victims," he declared. "A connection not only linking them together, but showing a common motive covering all three murders as well. We'll have to go back to the beginning of the series and start hunting for it."

"I've already hunted till my nerves are frazzled and my brain gone fuzzy," the inspector protested. "There isn't any connection! Cyril Kenwick, Nora Munday, and Hilary Thorp's servant never so much as saw one another."

"So far as you know," his friend quietly amended. "Yet it stands to reason their lives must have touched somewhere—unless we're dealing with a homicidal maniac who picked his victims at random."

"I've been tempted to accept that theory," Fisk glumly admitted. "The whole series seems so purposeless. Nobody even benefits financially, for none of the three had any money."

"No need of accepting a hypothetical maniac until we've exhausted every possibility of a reasonable motive," Traherne insisted. "One trouble is you've had too little time to thoroughly work out the clews. Young Kenwick died a week ago this evening, Nora Munday three days later and Duncan only last night. The inside of a week is too short a time for any one man to solve three murder mysteries, even with the help of his entire department. Suppose you let me give you a hand now? If you like I'll start at the beginning and re-cover the ground on my own."

"Good idea," Fisk approved. "You've met very few of the people involved and can bring a new viewpoint to bear on each group. Want a blanket letter covering the fact that you're working with me?"

"Yes, and I'd better have it now." Traherne glanced at his watch. "No time like the present; I'll pay the Kenwick house a visit before dinner."

"I meant asking you to explore some of Gentsy Judd's pet night clubs with me—if my men can't locate him I've got to take a hand myself."

"Sorry, but I'll be more useful working alone. Give me a ring any time to-night if you've news, or want me."

"Apparently the fact that we had no sleep last night hasn't bred a wild craving for bed." The prospect of Traherne's active cooperation had already cast a cheerful glow over the inspector's hitherto pessimistic mood. "Sit tight for five minutes and I'll write you the covering letter."

In visiting the Kenwick house, however, Traherne made no use of it. He had served an apprenticeship as character actor before the days of successful playwrighting and chose to cultivate the Kenwick butler on the plane of a fellow servant rather than officially. For the part no actual make-up was needed; instead a change of clothing and way of brushing the hair, together with an even more drastic alteration of voice and manner enabled Traherne to impersonate a dignified upper-grade servant drawn by curiosity—thinly veiled under the excuse of seeking advice about neighboring markets—into visiting a fellow-butler whose position in the Kenwick household made him a source of possibly thrilling inside information.

Barnabus, the only man in a house otherwise served by women, was only too glad to welcome a person of his own impeccable social standing, and they promptly foregathered in his roomy pantry over a pot of delicious tea. The question of markets once cursorily disposed of, Traherne felt it safe to reveal his much deeper interest in the famous murder case and Barnabus showed not the slightest hesitancy about embarking on an orgy of confidential gossip.

"As you say you're new to the neighborhood you likely don't know what a queer family we've always been." He passed the visitor a plate of lavishly buttered crumpets, then stirred his own tea with the contented air of one settling to an hour of pleasant relaxation from the serious cares of life. "Personally I can't speak of the time when Mrs. Kenwick was alive, but I'm told it was a queer family even then, though nothing to what it's been since. What with the father going clean daft on religion—not that church isn't a very good thing in its way, of course—and the son taking to the bottle in his teens as natural as a duck to water. What with both of them hating each other like sin and never more lively company than church deacons and wardens invited inside our doors, it's not what you'd call cheerful service."

"I wonder you've stuck it so long. The papers say you've been in the family for years."

"Oh, there are compensations; the old gentleman's generous with his money and not too strict an eye kept on how it's spent. It's only since Mr. Cyril got keeping company with this divorced lady of his that real trouble started. The old gentleman's death on divorce."

"You saw this Mrs. Tabour at the inquest?" Traherne interestedly inquired. "I was there myself and thought her a pretty piece, but tricky—would she have aught to do with his death, do you think?"

"It's my belief the old gentleman's right, in a manner of speaking, when he says it was only the Lord had a hand in that. Not that I think he struck the poor lad down of a purpose, it's only that you can't drink come early, come late, with never a let-up. Nobody's stomach wouldn't stand it!"

"So much liquor had given the young gentleman bad health then?"

"He'd been ailing for weeks past—it's likely some drink not quite what it should be put the finishing touch and sent him off."

"But at the inquest their family doctor said nothing about Mr. Cyril's being sick."

Something in the apparently innocent remark slew Barnabus' enjoyment of their gossipy chat, he almost visibly retired into a shell of reserve.

"Doctors are mostly a close-mouthed crew. And now, I hope you'll not take it amiss if I say I've duties that need attending. If there's anything else I can tell you of the tradespeople hereabouts I'd be most glad to oblige some other time."

Traherne accepted the dismissal with a slightly offended dignity which he felt well in character, then, when Barnabus had shown him out through the basement door, carefully memorized the sentence that had so abruptly dried up the butler's font of information at its very source. "But at the inquest their family doctor said nothing about Mr. Cyril's being sick." Now, what fact concerning Cyril's health lay heavy on the good Barnabus' conscience? And did he know more about the mysterious poison than he had so far told?

It was too late to make the necessary alterations in his appearance and still make the next call on his mental list before the hour at which most New Yorkers dine, so Traherne enjoyed a leisurely meal and then telephoned to Shirley Tabour asking if she would receive an out-of-town journalist who was anxious to secure a really authentic account of the famous poison mysteries for his home paper.

If there was one thing Shirley could never willingly forego it was an opportunity to talk with an interesting male of the species, and Sydney Traherne possessed an attractive telephone-voice; she announced herself as at home and disengaged. Her first sight of the out-of-town journalist was a trifle disappointing for no one could call Traherne exactly handsome, but by way of compensation his technique in the way of subtly administered flattery was unsurpassed; in half an hour Shirley had mentally voted him well worth while.

At his request she presently went over the story of her engagement to Cyril Kenwick from its inception to the time of its breaking on the last afternoon of his life, while Traherne vainly listened for some hint of an enlightening clew. Cross questioned regarding Cyril's health she protested entire ignorance, he had never mentioned the subject as far as she could remember.

Finally they arrived at the cocktail-drinking episode of the fatal Sunday afternoon. Shirley insisted all her ingredients had been above suspicion, also everything but the orange juice was afterwards analyzed by headquarter chemists.

"There wasn't any of that left over," she explained. "But of course there couldn't be anything wrong with oranges bought at an ordinary fruit stand."

"You and your cousin felt no ill effects?"

"I didn't, and I'm not sure if Fay drank any. She was in the pantry while I mixed the third or fourth cocktail, but I don't remember if she took any."

Now this was the first the investigators had heard of Fay's nearness to the suspect cocktail shaker, and Traherne wondered if his inclination to exonerate her was a mistaken one.

"Haven't I read that you and Cyril Kenwick were entirely alone?"

"Yes, and it's perfectly true. When I told Fay I was breaking our engagement she decided not to appear until after Cyril had gone. We've kept her name out of the papers as much as possible because her husband's such a horrid crank, and the inspector has been ever so nice and understanding, he's hardly mentioned Fay at all."

"I'm afraid I hear a bell ringing somewhere." Traherne was gifted with unusually acute hearing and the conversation had reached a stage at which he welcomed interruption.

"Oh, bother! it's the front door bell," Shirley announced after a second's attentive listening. "I'll have to answer it myself for my maid's out."

She left the door wide open so that he could hear her high heels tapping along the passage and catch her surprised exclamation at the door.

"For the love of Mike, what are you doing here?"

A masculine voice answered with some undistinguishable phrase that failed to reach Traherne, then the door closed and Shirley returned, followed by a stout, rather dissipated looking man in a most elaborate costume.

"Of all things, here's my late lamented ex. come to call!" She laughingly introduced the two men. "Here's where you *do* land a scoop for your hick paper—he hasn't been to see me since the divorce."

"It's practically a visit of condolence," Jerome Tabour rather gingerly accepted one of the spindly gold chairs, seeming to doubt its ability to sustain his weight. "Seeing that we're both mixed up in murder cases I came to suggest burying the hatchet and sort of bucking each other up—reunion of mutual sympathy idea, for there seems no telling which of us is booked to be first on the inside looking out."

"Brute! I don't know an earthly thing about your private murder case, but in mine there's not the least chance of my being accused."

Traherne caught himself wondering if it was customary for divorced wives to so frankly turn the battery of their wiles on unexpectedly appearing ex-husbands; did the fact that a man was no longer a co-wearer of the marriage yoke enhance his value?

"Don't be too sure you're swimming free of suspicion," Jerome Tabour darkly advised. "I've heard more than one insinuation against your cocktails."

"Then show you're a sport and don't believe a word of it by letting me mix you an extra special one," Shirley gayly suggested.

"Sure it's safe? This talking over old times is a thirsty business, but I'd hate going the way of all flesh."

"Old times aren't going to enter in," she assured him. "We'll play we're two innocents persecuted by murder-investigators, who've just met for the first time and plan drowning their woes in the best synthetic gin ever disguised to resemble the genuine article. What say?"

"I'm with you." The ex-husband grinned at her reminiscently. "You always did shake a wicked cocktail!"

Traherne stayed long enough to sample the first fruit of Shirley's bar-tending ability, then left them to what he half suspected would end in a reconciliation between the rather spicy pair.

Altogether he had spent more than two hours in Shirley's apartment with the only net result, so far as he could see, discovery of the fact that Fay Redmond had been close to her cousin's cocktail shaker with a probable opportunity to tamper with its contents before Cyril Kenwick drank his share. Still, if there had been anything wrong with the mixture why had Shirley Tabour suffered no ill effects? In face of her immunity it seemed safe to conclude that if Cyril had been poisoned in Shirley's apartment it must have been by means of the glass from which he drank rather than the cocktail itself.

Though the night was still young, judging by New York standards, he decided against starting on the next lap of his lone-hand inquiry until next morning. So far he had spent too little time in carefully weighing available evidence, for up to the time of Zoe Panza's

visit and his own abrupt entry into the case, he had turned a slightly inattentive ear to Inspector Fisk's accounts of the investigation. It was the third murder coming so close on the heels of the other two that had finally impelled him into temporary desertion of his play in favor of active cooperation with his sorely tried friend.

Arrived at the apartment building where he lived Traherne exchanged a word or two with the doorman, then went directly up to the seventh floor. Always in the habit of moving quietly, he made very little noise in passing along the corridor and opening his own apartment door, then, as his hand went out toward the light switch it was arrested by a faint sound coming from the rear of the apartment. The half-extended hand dropped at his side and for a moment or so he stood listening intently, before tiptoeing through the passageway leading to his study.

The study itself was dark and apparently empty but from the small laboratory beyond came sounds of subdued movement; he could hear an indistinct rustle and a click suggesting the closing of a latch. The blinds at both study windows were drawn down shutting out any glimmer of reflected light from the city, but once he had stealthily crossed it and gained the laboratory door he could see that its single window was wide open, admitting a dim radiance barely strong enough to show him a boyish figure crouching against a built-in cabinet where he kept various instruments and chemicals needed in his laboratory work. A lower compartment was open, with the ray of a flashlight playing inquisitively over its contents.

"So you took the bait."

With the words his finger touched the wall button, flooding the room with light and revealing a very much startled Zoe Panza who gained her feet in one lithe spring.

"It was a trap, then?" Her big black eyes blazed defiantly.

"Rather a test. Just as Inspector Fisk mentioned a basket-work case I heard some one outside the door and not knowing who it was, supplied some misleading information as to the present whereabouts of a certain queer little case. Of course when you came in a couple of seconds later I knew it was you I'd heard, but wasn't sure whether to assign your listening pause to simple curiosity or a deeper interest in an article only Fisk and I knew about."

Suddenly Zoe's tense expression broke into the curly-lipped smile that seemed to hold so much more mirth than the smiles of other people.

"Just the sort of trick you would play on a poor defenseless reporter!" she accused. "Naturally, once I knew you and Conway Fisk were suppressing something made of basket-work I couldn't resist trying to find out what it was. You said you meant examining it to-morrow so it had to be got at before then, and of course I didn't expect you'd come home at such an unholy early hour! Don't I make a nice boy?"

She rose on tiptoe, slowly revolving that he might better admire her masculine garb.

"What's the idea of the change in sex?"

"Well, as you've probably guessed," her eyes flashed to the open window, "I came down from the roof by way of the fire escape; skirts wouldn't have made the descent any easier. Besides, in a big building like this no one pays much attention to a mere boy; girls get looked at with a more discerning and remembering eye."

"But suppose you'd been caught? The disguise might have landed you in serious trouble."

"Why cross one's bridges while they're still in the distance? I'd have sworn I was only taking you up on a dare and trusted to you're not giving me away."

"Confiding disposition, haven't you?" He found it next to impossible to be really angry with the girl no matter how outrageously she behaved. "Come on into my study and I'll give you a drink while we discuss the best way of smuggling you out unobserved."

"Aren't you going to be a darling and show me this mysterious case?"

"I am not. You may see and hear about it later on, but at present it's a dark secret."

"That's why I'm aching for just a glimpse."

"Come and have the ache cured by a glass of really decent sherry."

"The cruelty of the man! As if alcohol could console me!"

She nevertheless accepted his liquid hospitality with a good grace once she felt sure he had no intention of weakening in his refusal to show her the basket-work case.

"How's your patient?" Traherne asked, holding a match for her cigarette.

"Patient? Oh, Teddy! Isn't he a dear? and His car's so useful to run about in. Too bad he has to go back to work to-morrow so I can only make use of him after office hours. By the way, I presented the inspector's card and met Fay Redmond this afternoon; rather a beauty, don't you think?"

"I don't pretend to be a connoisseur. Did you also meet her husband?"

"Yes, and—he most emphatically didn't like me!"

To Traherne's amazement her voice held a thrill of unmistakable pain, while the big black eyes suddenly dropping to her stiffly extended hands glittered oddly. Only later did he guess the significance of tone and gesture. At the time he only wondered why her otherwise perfect taste failed her in the matter of fingernails; they were stained with an almost vermilion liquid polish, a hideous color that hid the natural tint and did its best to mar the beauty of the small flexible hands.

"He didn't strike me as a person given to liking people." His casual comment brought her back to her normal self.

"A sarcastic old beast! He practically showed me the door."

"If that's all he did I can go you one better; he not only showed it to me, I thought he was going to kick me out."

"No wonder his poor wife looks meek. But do you know—please don't think me a frightful cat—I always feel tempted to distrust women who look so obtrusively virtuous? I wonder if she isn't hiding some lurid secrets?"

12

At about the time Zoe Panza and her involuntary host settled to a confidential talk, Conway Fisk commenced his personal hunt for the missing Gentsy Judd. Knowing the vanished cracksman's favorite haunts only woke to active life after midnight he had snatched a few hours needed sleep, then started a round of visits to various night clubs, landing just before three a.m. in an establishment known as the Dancing Bat.

It was a place surreptitiously catering, behind its outer cloak of dancing and exorbitant suppers, more to hard gamblers than hard drinkers, and one which never so far had come into active conflict with the police, largely because of its usefulness as a known resort of higher-class crooks. If a certain cracksman or forger was wanted on short notice he was more likely to be found at the Dancing Bat than anywhere else; a fact which had brought Fisk in spite of his man's report that no one had recently seen Gentsy Judd there.

Tired, but persistent, the inspector talked with one underworld acquaintance after another without gaining any news of his quarry. It hardly seemed possible that the cracksman had escaped the city before a general police alarm was sent out, yet if he was still within its limits he must be lying very low indeed.

Just as Fisk decided on abandoning his quest, for that night at least, an ex-cardsharp who now claimed to be an entirely reformed character stopped at his table.

"Hear you're looking for Gentsy Judd, inspector."

"No need of publishing my connection with the police," Fisk retorted. "And if you've anything to tell me sit down; it attracts less attention." He beckoned a passing waiter and ordered coffee as an excuse for continued occupancy of a table. "Now, what do you know?"

"Not a thing. I only wanted to point out Gentsy's best frail to you, she most probably knows where he is."

"I doubt it, but there's no harm trying. Can we see her from here?"

"Not while she's sitting down. Next time she dances I'll point her out."

She was a sickly, yellow-haired little creature, whom Fisk almost instantly guessed to be a drug addict. They watched her pass their table twice during the next dance number, and when it was finished Conway Fisk was duly piloted across to her table and introduced. At first "Trixie," as the ex-card sharp called her, was inclined toward suspicion of the stranger, but her coolness thawed under his offer to stand supper for the party.

During the meal and a following dance or two, the inspector complaisantly flattered himself that Trixie accepted him as an ordinary frequenter of the Dancing Bat—then, as they danced past a half open door she abruptly guided him through it and once beyond range of observant eyes, dropped his arm.

"We can talk in here." They were in a private dining-room, its disordered table showing it had been occupied earlier in the evening. "I know you're a bull and you're after Gentsy, but you got his number chalked all wrong."

"Know where he is?" Fisk made no attempt to deny his errand or identity.

"Not where he is, but I'm here to tell you where he wasn't."

"Sounds a bit involved. Exactly what are you trying to say?"

The girl shivered suddenly. "Give me a smoke and let's sit down—I don't feel so good."

"One doesn't—between shots," his tone was grim.

"Oh, stow it! What's it to do with you!" she flared indignantly, then crossed to drop into a chair, both thin elbows on the disordered table. "You aren't in the narcotic squad—homicide's your racket."

"How do you know?"

"It doesn't matter. You're after Gentsy for that Thorp robbery, ain't you?"

"If you can you'd better get word to him he'd be wiser to come forward and face the music—"

"Oh, yes? And likely get framed!" she jeered. "If you were any kind of a dick you wouldn't have picked on Gentsy for that job. He's a clean worker, he never kills!"

"There's always a first time—" Fisk had begun when she again cut him short.

"Well, he didn't do it, see? Why, he wasn't even in town."

"Is that the truth?"

"Yes. And what's more, I can prove it!" She made no attempt to hide her triumph.

"How? It'll take some pretty trustworthy evidence," Fisk warned.

"Yes? Well, ain't it true a camera can't lie?"

"A camera?"

"Sure." She giggled at his puzzled expression. "This Thorp job was pulled last night, wasn't it? Well, on Friday some big-wig landed in Montreal, Canada, and Pathé weekly took a shot at him getting off the train. Go look up the news reel yourself and you'll see Gentsy, big as life, all mixed up in the crowd. Suppose he didn't know the camera was spotting him but he's there all right, I saw the film this afternoon."

"He *could* have got back in time for a Saturday night job," the inspector pointed out. "Does the news reel show him getting off the train?"

"Sure. He's one of a bunch that gets off before the bigwig shows up."

"Humph, doesn't sound probable that he'd take such a long trip, then turn round and come directly back," Fisk mused aloud. "Hadn't you better tell me what took him to Canada?"

Trixie appeared to debate the point, finally deciding that a measure of frankness was her wisest policy.

"I'll say it sounds fishy, but honest to God somebody paid Gentsy to skip the state. Since I heard you dicks were after him I've wondered if it wasn't done so the real thief could pin the Thorp job on Gentsy and he mightn't be able to prove where he was so he couldn't come back and give 'em the lie."

"I half believe you're right."

"Is that honest?"

"It is."

"Well, I've heard you're a straight shooter—and just for that I'll tell you something else, I know where a girl you're looking for is; also why she did a bunk."

"What girl?"

"This Shirley Tabour's maid."

"Say, look here," Fisk was becoming seriously interested. "Exactly how much about this case do you know?"

"Only bits here and there," Trixie assured him. "Just enough to guess there's some kind of dirty work going on. Slithers could tell you more, but he's being paid to talk out of one side of his mouth, and he's no respect for the truth anyhow."

Fisk suppressed a smile at her indignant tone, then inquired: "Why did Shirley Tabour's maid fade off the scene?"

"Because she's a police record and knew you people wouldn't believe she was running straight. Once you caught her so close to a murder you'd be certain to make things hot for the poor kid."

"Do you know if she's any suspicion who killed Cyril Kenwick?"

"She says not—it was only the police record that made her run; she's done time for shoplifting."

"Well," Fisk considered the situation, "suppose you ask her to report at headquarters and insist on seeing me. Tell her I'll see the past isn't raked up, I simply want to question her about those infernal cocktails, and it's possible she knows something that has more meaning for us than for her."

"I'll pass the word," Trixie promised. "Now, let's go back to the others, I don't want 'em to think I've turned stool-pigeon."

"Say we've been having an extra drink," he advised. "And when you hear from Gentsy tell him we'll make it worth his while to give us the name of who ever bribed him to leave town."

"I'll do that little thing."

As they left the private dining-room they very narrowly escaped collision with two tall, rather unsteady old gentlemen; brothers, to judge by their marked resemblance to each other.

"A thousand pardons, Madame, a thousand pardons, sir!" They bowed with wavering but elaborate apology, their tightly linked arms lending mutual support as they straightened and wove an uncertain way across the polished floor.

"Beautifully lit," the inspector half smiled. "Who are they?"

"Everybody calls 'em the Palmer twins and nobody ever saw 'em cold sober," Trixie giggled. "They keep explaining they're only brothers, not twins at all, but it makes no difference, they get called twins just the same. It's a wonder you don't know them, they're jazzing round town most nights."

"Don't remember to have seen them before," the Inspector answered abstractedly—he had just caught sight of a couple whose entrance, together, quite extinguished his passing interest in the inebriated old gentlemen. Jerome Tabour and Shirley! What on earth were they celebrating in such intimate and hilarious good fellowship?

The showroom of the wholesale dress house which had employed Nora Munday as a model was hardly opened next morning when Sydney Traherne appeared, this time as Inspector Fisk's representative. Luckily it was the off season and only two of the showroom booths occupied by out-of-town buyers to whom the line was being shown, so that Nora's friend, Mildred Daily, could be spared for a talk with Traherne. They retired to an end booth, and offering the girl a cigarette, he settled to the task of discovering if she was not unconsciously holding back some scrap of information that might aid in solving the mystery of Nora Munday's murder.

After more than half an hour spent in listening to everything Mildred could recall about the dead model's habits, friends, tastes, he had almost despaired of finding any helpful clew amid so much irrelevant detail, when a chance remark from her set his ears again hopefully a-prick.

"Too bad she didn't feel sick enough to stop work and go home that last afternoon, if she had maybe she'd be alive now."

"That's the first time you've spoken of any illness."

"Is it? Well, I knew it couldn't have anything to do with her dying," Mildred explained. "You see, Nora used to read aloud to her father lots of evenings and perhaps she hadn't too good a light, anyway her eyes troubled her and sometimes she'd have awful headaches—she had one Wednesday afternoon."

"Were they ever bad enough to send her home?"

"Once in a while, not often. Her landlady said the headaches came from Nora's eyes being tired, and suggested her going to an oculist for some kind of treatment."

"Do you know if she went?"

"I'm not sure, maybe the landlady could tell you."

The Mundays' boarding place was in any case next on Traherne's schedule. First paying a visit to Howard Munday himself, he then asked for a private interview with the landlady who betrayed no hesitancy; she was beginning to rather count on any strangers who came to see the bereaved father afterwards donating a substantial sum toward his support.

Cross-examined about the state of Nora's health just previous to her death the woman insisted there had been nothing wrong with it; she had never heard Nora complain of any kind of ache or pain. Had her eyes troubled her? Not so far as the landlady knew. It was not until Traherne, pretending to a much greater knowledge than he actually possessed, threatened her with police prosecution that the woman broke down, tearfully confessing that she had been bribed to send Nora to a certain oculist.

Asked for a description of the person offering the bribe she could only tell him it was a woman who had called one evening just about dusk, seeming more incapable than unwilling to furnish anything like a description of the unknown female. After many tearful protests that she had meant no harm at all in accepting the proffered money, Traherne finally drove her into hunting for the card bearing the name and address of the eye specialist whom she had been paid to recommend to Nora. It proved hard to find but was at length run to earth in a dusty pigeon-hole of her desk, and, seeing that it carried a nearby address, Traherne drove the two or three intervening blocks meaning to at least have a look at the oculist who employed such unusual methods for securing patients.

The number he was looking for decorated the door of a ramshackle old building, remodeled into tiny apartments, several of which were for rent. Nowhere could he see signs of an oculist's office.

Prolonged ringing finally brought a slovenly janitor or caretaker to the door, and from him Fisk learned that Dr. Davis had closed his office and moved away on the preceding Thursday, the very day as his questioner instantly realized, on which Nora Munday's body was identified in the morgue. The janitor's description of the departed oculist was almost as vague as that supplied by Nora's landlady of the offerer of the bribe; still one fact did appear to have fixed itself in the man's foggy mind, he was sure his late tenant's hair had been black, very black and very smooth.

"Thinking it over, every second man connected with the case seems to be black-haired," Traherne disgustedly reflected as he drove away from the oculist's empty nest. "Jerome Tabour has it, likewise Teddy Thorp, Joel Redmond, this stool-pigeon, Slithers, and, come to think of it, Conway Fisk!"

Upon which latter thought he chuckled softly, then headed for his next destination in a slightly more cheerful mood.

It was one of the clear spring days which atone for much evil in the way of New York's winter climate, an ideal day for his run out to the road house where Jerome Tabour had taken Nora to dinner.

13

It was an unbelievable tableau on which Shirley Tabour's eyes lighted as she paused, transfixed, on the threshold of her own pink and gold drawing-room. Fay, in the arms of a white-haired man who was obviously not her husband! It simply wasn't possible, she must be seeing things!

Shirley regretfully remembered the highly exuberant state in which she had retired at some vaguely grayish hour that morning, then dug two plump pink fists into her eyes rubbing with a vigor calculated to dispel any hazy lingering of over-night fog. At the same instant another sense bore witness that the love scene was real; Fay's soft, distressed voice keyed to a passionate note her cousin had never heard before.

"Alan, let me go, dear—we mustn't, it's desperately wrong!"

And a second voice which Shirley numbly recognized as belonging to Dr. Munro, answered:

"Love such as ours is never wrong, beloved!"

They were neither of them aware of the pajamaed vision on the threshold. Shirley quietly drew a fraction further back into the hall and shamelessly listened.

"Always I have borne in my heart the ache of incurable loneliness—have drifted through life a shadow among other flitting shadows that never found admittance to the sealed place wherein my soul shivered in icy solitude. Then, from out the myriad ghost-shapes peopling the world, came one at whose touch the seals fell broken, the chill of solitude was warmed, the leaden weight against my heart forever lifted! Can you marvel that to that one I give devotion such as weaker men bestow upon consoling gods?"

"Oh, hush! Please hush," Fay implored. "It is wrong for you to speak so, doubly wrong for me to listen! We must remember that I am not free—my husband loves me!"

"Love! Why defame so precious a word by pinning it to the selfish, exacting passion of a withered cynic for the pure white flesh and tender blood of a girl-wife more his prey than his companion? Can you look squarely into my eyes and tell me you return this thing you call his love?"

Rather breathlessly Shirley watched the man's gentle but compelling hands frame Fay's face between them, lifting it until she could no longer avoid meeting his splendid, dark-lashed eyes.

For long seconds it seemed to Fay she drowned in lakes of molten blue fire that burned away defenses, scorched to a blackened cinder her resistant sense of duty, and left her with body and lips that craved only complete surrender.

Neither of them saw nor heard Shirley as she turned to tiptoe softly away, her mind rather dazed and very much aggrieved. Of all the men who had made love to her not one had ever spoken in a voice of such passion-laden music, not one had talked about his solitary soul or held her with precisely that mixture of mastery and reverence. She went back to her interrupted toilet feeling there was something very much askew with the world in general and her own reconciliation with Jerome Tabour in particular.

At about the same hour that afternoon Inspector Fisk reached a similar conclusion as to the general perversity of the universe, though his opinion was based upon quite different data. He had received a visit from Shirley

Tabour's missing maid and felt satisfied that the girl really knew nothing of Cyril Renwick's murder and had only run away because of her police record; various telegraph and telephone messages sent and received from Montreal, Canada, proved that Gentsy Judd was still in the city and could bring plenty of reliable witnesses to swear he hadn't left it since his arrival there on Friday; the stool-pigeon, Slithers, stuck like a limpet to his original story, both as to information gathered from the inspector's last night's acquaintance, Trixie, and the fact that no one but Teddy Thorp had entered or left the Thorp house during Zoe Panza's absence; and, as a crowning injury, he had heard nothing from Sydney Traherne all day and had failed in all attempts to get into touch with him.

"Taken by and large, it's one hell of a case," he confided to his half-smoked cigar, "without one decent clew, or motive, or even a poison that the doctors can put a name to. Homicidal maniac—that'll turn out the answer, mark my word!"

He was still wallowing in pessimistic gloom when Sydney Traherne turned up half an hour later, and the latter's abstracted manner did nothing to cheer him.

"Believe I'm on the track of something, Fisk, but as yet it's too nebulous for publication." Traherne prowled restlessly about the office instead of settling to a friendly exchange of news and opinions. "A lot depends on the answer to a question: was there a rubber band on Duncan's third finger?"

"There was." The inspector's curiosity cocked a hopeful ear but the question was not followed by any enlightening confidences.

"Thanks." Traherne's brindled head nodded briefly. "There was a sheet over Duncan's body while you and I examined the jewel room—I stupidly neglected looking at his hands."

He took something from an inner pocket and tossed it across the desk. "What do you make of that?"

"Looks like two watch crystals glued together by some kind of paste spread round the edges." The inspector twisted it this way and that, but failed to see anything more than he had already described.

"Haven't you a magnifying glass?" Traherne asked, without ceasing his soft-footed prowl.

Fisk silently produced one, discovering that when subjected to its enlargement the small round crystals were no longer quite empty—several tiny bright green filaments sprayed irregularly from a common center.

"What are they?" He glanced inquiringly at Traherne. "Some new kind of deadly germ?"

"No, of themselves they're perfectly harmless."

"But what *are* they?" Fisk wanted to know.

"That's more than I can say with any certainty. They were caught on the inner sides of the little basket-work case we found in Hilary Thorp's jewel room. At a guess I'd call them minute hairs."

"Hairs? of that bright green color?" Fisk scoffed.

"Well, fasten any name you like to them," his friend generously offered. "And by the bye, I imagine they're scheduled as one of the important exhibits at somebody's forthcoming trial."

For several days Inspector Fisk found his horizon bounded by inquests, funerals, and routine work that lacked all concrete result. Gentlemen of the press continued to scathingly denounce a police force incapable of solving the mystery of the Perfumed Death which had already claimed three victims and might be expected to at any moment strike down a fourth unless something was done in the way of safeguarding a long-suffering public.

Even Sydney Traherne seemed to have deserted him. After his brief visit on Monday afternoon nothing more was heard from him and telephoning his apartment brought no satisfaction; each time his man simply stated that Mr. Traherne was out and had left no word as to when he would return.

Toward the end of the week Fisk's sorely tried patience wore so thin that action of some sort became imperative and he cast about for any line of inquiry not already followed to a bitter ending, either in murky quicksands of uncertainty or against a blank wall.

Presently remembering Traherne's remark that somewhere there was an overlooked clew pointing to a connection between the various poison victims, and that he meant going back to the beginning to search for it, Fisk decided on following the same procedure. He would start by minutely requestioning David Kenwick, his butler Barnabus, and, in fact, the entire household. A plan which, once formed, he put into instant execution.

He had been some little time in the Kenwick house and was deep in cross-examining its much-annoyed owner, when Barnabus entered to announce that a gentleman was calling to see Inspector Fisk. "A Mr. Tureen, I think, is the name, sir." It was near enough for Fisk to guess the caller's probable identity and he allowed the old gentleman to follow his manifest inclination and leave the library by one door as Sydney Traherne was shown in by another.

"Headquarters told me you'd left word this would be your first stop," he explained, "so I took a chance on catching you."

"It's about time you showed signs of life. I was beginning to think you'd left for a pleasure trip in parts unknown."

"Quite the contrary. The trailing of that elusive 'something' I mentioned had entailed plenty of hard work."

"Intend confiding where the trail ended?"

"It hasn't, that's the trouble." Traherne's brows were drawn into a puzzled, almost angry frown. "So far I've only reached a stage of fair certainty that I'm on the right track, without a particle of tangible evidence to prove it. But, unless my deductions are completely wrong, we need to guard against a fourth murder—ever hear of two wealthy old gentlemen so inseparable that they're known as the Palmer twins?"

"I've not only heard of them, I've seen them," was the inspector's response. "They're patrons of a night club favored by Gentsy Judd, and I ran into them, almost literally, while looking for him."

"So? Well, it's Lloyd Palmer, the younger of the two, whom I think's in danger. Will you drive up to their house with me, now, and issue an official warning?"

"If you like, but can't you first give me an inkling what it's all about?" Fisk eyed his friend with rapidly-mounting curiosity.

"I'd sooner warn Lloyd Palmer first; we can talk after he understands what threatens him."

"You must think the danger pretty close."

"I do."

Inspector Fisk had reached for his hat when, after a discreet tap, Barnabus opened the door to say that he was wanted on the phone. While he answered it Conway Fisk restlessly paced the long room, his eyes constantly seeking the clock as if for reassurance that the wait was really only a matter of minutes. Four of them had ticked into eternity before Fisk returned, his face gone haggard in the brief interval.

"We're too late, Syd. That was Fay Redmond phoning from the Palmer house to say they've just found Lloyd Palmer in his car—dead!"

"How did she know you were here?" Traherne shot the question as they hurriedly left the house.

"Through headquarters, precisely as you yourself did."

They had descended the front steps and were halfway across the sidewalk when Fisk's roving eye lit on a tall brisk figure leaving a house two or three doors away.

"There's Dr. Munro—why not take him with us?" he suggested. "We'll probably need a physician to attend whatever ladies there are in the Palmer family."

Traherne only nodded a preoccupied assent and the inspector waited for Dr. Munro, who was already coming toward them. A few words explained their errand and the doctor heartily welcomed the chance of accompanying them.

"You know the address?" Fisk asked his friend as the car slid smoothly toward Fifth avenue.

Traherne merely nodded without emerging from the frowning preoccupation which the others respected until human curiosity refused further repression.

"Hadn't you better post me as to what you've discovered—or suspect?" Fisk finally inquired.

"Sorry, but it's all too tangled to permit anything like a coherent summing up." Traherne still spoke absently, all but the surface of his mind busy with fitting this latest development into its proper place.

After that they let him alone, Fisk and the doctor talking in low tones and the latter showing decided uneasiness when told it was Fay Redmond who had telephoned the news.

"I've never heard her mention these Palmers," he fumed. "How desperately unfortunate that she happened to be in their house to-day, of all days!"

"She does seem to possess an unlucky habit of being on the spot, or close to it, when there's murder about," the inspector commented rather dryly. "This is the third time, if we include her visit to Hilary Thorp a few hours before Duncan was killed."

"It's outrageous to even hint at anything beyond coincidence!" Dr. Munro's fine eyes shot sparks of indignant blue flame. "If you knew Fay as well as I do, you'd realize it's not only outrageous, but absurd. She could no more be a party to anything criminal than—than an angel stepped down from Heaven."

"Exactly how well do you know her?"

At which question the silver-haired doctor blushed like a schoolboy, and retired into offended silence.

As they swung into the crosstown block containing the Palmer house they could see a fair-sized crowd already collected around a coupé over which two uniformed policemen stood guard. Inspector Fisk was known to both men, who hailed his appearance with open relief.

"We've had our work keeping the crowd back, sir, but one of the ladies said you were on the way and we knew nothing must be touched till you got here."

"How did you come on the scene?"

"A maidservant ran to the corner and fetched me off my beat," one of the policemen explained. "McGuire here, just spotted the crowd and turned up to lend me a hand."

"Where are the ladies?"

"I got them to go inside—one lady pretty near fainted and we already had our hands full."

"Very wise to get them indoors. Now, keep people back while we have a look."

The guarded coupé was not driven accurately in against the curb, instead the inner front wheel had climbed to the sidewalk and both rear wheels slurred off at an angle suggesting the driver's lack of entire control.

"Hm-m—" Fisk inspected the car's position before examining the huddled figure sagging across the steering wheel. "Looks as if his eye or hand had failed him so he didn't turn soon enough and ran spank into the curb."

He went closer, peering in through the open left window. In slumping forward the old man's head had twisted sideways so that it lay almost in the wheel's center, the gray, ghastly face turned full toward the open window. One arm hung at his side, the other sprawled stiffly over the wheel while about the third finger of its helplessly drooping hand a narrow rubber band was loosely twisted.

"You might take a look at him, Dr. Munro," Fisk suggested, "though I think there's no doubt he's dead."

As the doctor complied a small roadster came honking down the block, dead against the one-way arrow; a violation of traffic regulations so flagrant that even their more serious duty failed to blind Patrolman McGuire. He stepped into the street, bent on rebuking the impertinent car, and was very nearly run over for his pains. The roadster missed him by inches as it swung smoothly into place behind the already parked car and Zoe Panza jumped lightly out, leaving Teddy Thorp to explain his reckless driving to the irate policeman. She was as bright-eyed and beamingly sure of a welcome as usual, quite refusing to be daunted by the inspector's protesting glare.

"Now, in the name of all that's Holy—how did you know there was anything happening here?" he resignedly inquired.

"Feminine intuition, inspector dear; it whispered of a sudden death, a possible murder—naturally, in the interest of my paper—"

"Oh, damn your paper! That leak at headquarters will cost somebody their job yet."

"The man is undoubtedly dead." Dr. Munro had straightened from his brief examination of the body across the wheel, and now came close to where Traherne, Fisk and Zoe stood in a little group. "I suppose he must be left undisturbed until the medical examiner comes?"

"Yes, I'll phone him directly we go inside." Fisk turned to the police officers. "Can you carry on until he gets here?"

"Surely—" McGuire was beginning when his speech was checked by a wailing cry, almost a howl, from the house behind them.

"Lloyd! Lloyd!" A tall old man, whom Fisk recognized as one of the brothers he had seen at the Dancing Bat, half staggered, half fell across the sidewalk toward the parked car, reached it, and before any one could stop him seized the body by both shoulders, roughly shaking it while he sobbed wild protests and entreaties. "Lloyd—tell 'em it's not true—tell 'em you're not dead! Liars! puling swine, trying to frighten a poor old man; I'll teach 'em, I'll— I'll—" He lapsed into a choking gurgle made no less repulsive because of the genuine agony it voiced.

He was palpably drunk, almost to the point of collapse, yet he had succeeded in seriously disturbing the pose of his brother's dead body; a pose which might easily have furnished important indications had it been left as originally found. It was with slightly ungentle hands that Fisk caught the old man, dragging him away from the open car window.

"Better get him in the house. Take an arm, Traherne."

Between them they impelled the frantically resisting old gentleman toward the now open front door, where a dignified manservant stood awaiting them. As he reached accustomed hands for the now violently cursing inebriate Fisk resigned his part of the duty, pausing to cast a backward eye over the morbidly curious little crowd and the two blue uniforms keeping a cleared space around the death-car. Best leave the street situation to them.

"Come on, Dr. Munro. No—" as Zoe Panza darted confidently forward. "You stay outside, young lady. Cultivate patience and Teddy Thorp until we're ready to make a statement to the press."

14

From a room on the left of the wide hall came a sound of subdued weeping.

"Mrs. Palmer, sir," the manservant answered Fisk's inquiring look. "She's in there with Mrs. Redmond."

"Can you manage him alone?"

"Oh, yes, sir. I'd often to handle both brothers when drink got the best of them."

The inspector first phoned to headquarters, coroner, and medical examiner, then sent a maid who had appeared from behind a green baize door evidently leading to the domestic regions, to tell the ladies that he was obliged to question them without further delay.

"You'd better come with us, Dr. Munro," he added as the girl entered the room from which still filtered sounds of stifled weeping. "Lucky you have your medical case along." For the doctor had been on the point of starting for a round of visits when they collected him. "The tearful lady may need some kind of a dose. Is she the dead man's wife, Traherne? Or had he one?"

"I haven't the faintest idea." His friend's tone was still somewhat abstracted, as though an under-problem absorbed most of his thoughts.

When the three men entered the room on the left they relievedly discovered that no medical help was required;

Mrs. Palmer had choked back all outward signs of grief, facing them with a calmness only marred by the redness of her fine gray eyes.

"Good afternoon, Mrs. Redmond," the inspector addressed her with a certain formal politeness reserved for people whom he did not altogether trust. "Since you know us all, perhaps you'll be kind enough to vouch for us to—Mrs. Palmer?"

"Yes." Fay's eyes fled helplessly to Dr. Munro and clung to him as if begging support, a plea he answered by going to stand close beside her while she hurriedly introduced all three men to Mrs. Palmer.

"Sorry it's necessary to ask questions at a time like this," the inspector apologized, keenly scrutinizing Constance Palmer's delicate, ravaged face which once, he mentally noted, must have been extremely beautiful though time, and very probably her husband's habits, had now carved lines and hollows that robbed it of all save a certain twilit loveliness. "But the time element is always valuable. Who was it that first discovered your husband?"

"It was Fay who first noticed the car standing outside." Mrs. Palmer's voice was curiously unmodulated, almost as if she deliberately kept it on a toneless level. "James, the footman, went out to see what was wrong."

"Is he the servant who just now took charge of your brother-in-law?"

"I suppose so, we haven't other men in our employ."

"I shall need to question him presently. Now, suppose we start a bit further back—when did Mr. Palmer leave home?"

"Directly after luncheon."

"Was he quite in his usual health?"

"I think so."

"Did he say where he was going?"

"Oh, no, Lloyd seldom mentioned what he intended doing."

"He was not engaged in any form of business?"

"No. He and Bronson retired several years ago."

"Bronson is the brother?"

"Yes."

"The elder of the two?"

"By half a dozen years."

"I've been told they were practically inseparable—do you know why their habit of being always together was broken this afternoon?"

Constance Palmer hesitated, a shamed flush staining her almost ghastly pallor. "I imagine because—Bronson was asleep when my husband left."

"Asleep? At lunch time? Was he ill?"

"No. Simply sleeping off the effects of last night's debauch." In spite of her marvelous control a hint of bitterness edged the level voice.

"Bronson Palmer had been out alone last night, then?"

"On the contrary my husband was with him, but he could always carry liquor better than Bronson could; he recovered quicker from its effects."

"Do you know where they went last night?"

"No. I never know." There was a whole tragedy in the simple statement.

"Or at what time they returned home?"

"Not even that. Years ago I gave up listening for my husband's return."

"The brothers went out together every evening?"

"Not quite that. Sometimes they stayed at home and—caroused is the only term that describes their idea of a quiet evening spent at home."

"Now, coming back to to-day's luncheon; you say Mr. Palmer was quite well?"

"I imagine so, otherwise he would have complained."

"Please think carefully and tell me exactly what he ate."

She apparently did as he requested, the chronic frown between her delicately arched brows deepening until it was almost a scowl.

"It seems stupid, but I'm afraid I didn't notice," she presently declared. "Perhaps cook or the maid who waited on table can answer your question."

"At least you must know if Mr. Palmer ate of the same dishes that you did?"

"I didn't notice." Neither her voice nor face betrayed dislike of the topic, but Traherne, who had a habit of studying hands, saw that one of hers was so tightly clenched that the bones of the knuckles showed white.

Inspector Fisk made a note to question the servants regarding precisely what food or drink Lloyd Palmer had taken for luncheon, then passed on to another phase of the inquiry.

"Now, Mrs. Palmer, do you mind telling me just how you spent the afternoon?"

"I did nothing in particular. Only read for a while, then went over some household accounts and after that carried a tray of toast and tea up to Bronson's room. I was still there when Fay came."

Traherne saw that as she spoke the clenched hand relaxed; the change of subject had evidently relieved some secret tension.

"You expected her?"

"No."

"You and Mrs. Redmond are old friends, perhaps?"

"We've known one another ever since her marriage. Our husbands were in business together then."

"And that was—how long ago?"

"Nearly eight years, I think." She glanced at Fay for confirmation.

"Quite eight." The younger woman answered her look.

"Now," the inspector returned to the main thread of cross-examination, "you left off with Mrs. Redmond's arrival. What happened then?"

"We went into the front drawing-room and, because she saw I was terribly nervous, Fay played and sang to me. Then Fay said a storm must be coming up, it was growing so dark she couldn't see the music properly. That's how she happened to notice Lloyd's car."

"Because she couldn't see her music?" He failed to quite catch the connection.

"Yes, of course. Fay went to the window to see if it really was getting ready to storm and the coupé was parked with some one sitting behind the wheel. She tapped on the window pane and waved, but when Lloyd didn't move she called me over and we both looked out."

"The windows are too high to give you a clear sight of the car's interior—how did you know the man at the wheel was your husband?"

"Why, who else could it have been? Fay and I both recognized the car, it's a peculiar shade of mauve, and Lloyd always drove it himself."

"So you sent the footman out to see what was wrong—" Fisk prompted.

"Not immediately—we—knew Lloyd's habits and thought he might be drunk. Then, after perhaps ten minutes' waiting to see if he'd move, I rang for James and told him to see if Mr. Palmer required help."

"Did you both remain at the window?"

"Yes. We saw James go to the car and, after a second or two, reach in through the open window and touch Lloyd's shoulder. He jumped back so oddly that we guessed something must be really wrong, for finding his master drunk wouldn't frighten James in the least. Fay and I both went out then, and as soon as we saw Lloyd's face we knew he was dead!"

"You neither of you actually touched him? Think carefully, it may prove important."

"I didn't. I've a nervous horror of death and there was no mistaking the expression of his face—only a dead person *could* look quite like that—but—" She paused, struggling to recall precisely what had happened during those first tragic seconds of discovery. "I think, in fact I'm almost sure, Fay leaned in through the window to make sure Lloyd was dead."

"And then?" Fisk again prompted.

"One of the maids ran out through the service door, she had seen us all on the sidewalk and knew there must be something wrong. Fay, or perhaps it was James, sent her for a policeman and—then my memory is a little confused, I think I must have come near fainting."

"Not much wonder in face of a shock like that." The inspector's tone was sympathetic. "Some one helped you into the house?"

"Yes, Fay. I remember hearing her tell James to watch the car until a policeman came."

"Thank you, Mrs. Palmer, you make an excellent witness with a quite unusual memory for details."

He studied his notes for a little, considering whether his questions had covered all the ground necessary at the moment. One or two points might require further probing, but for the present Constance Palmer appeared to have rendered all the assistance in her power. He turned to Fay Redmond, a sudden sternness replacing the almost gentle consideration with which he had treated the older woman.

"Now, Mrs. Redmond, perhaps you'll kindly tell us just how you always manage to be on, or very near, the scene whenever this Perfumed Death claims a victim?"

"Not Nora Munday!" Fay quickly denied; too quickly; her very haste betraying that her association with three out of the four poison victims had already occurred to her.

"Then you admit she's the only exception?"

"I—" Again Fay's eyes fled to Dr. Munro and his answering look of almost fanatic devotion restored her flagging courage; she faced the inspector with a new dignity. "Because I was in my cousin's apartment when Cyril Kenwick paid his last visit there—because I happened to sell Hilary Thorp a ruby a few hours before his house was robbed and his manservant killed—because I am here today visiting an old friend whom I often come to see—none of these things give you a right to use that tone, Inspector Fisk. If you could point to one instance in which I benefit in the slightest degree it might be different."

"You've put your finger on the thing that's saving you, young lady." Fisk solemnly nodded at her. "If I could find the shadowy ghost of a motive—"

"Well, you won't find one!" she openly defied.

"You realize your name can no longer be kept out of this? Not even to spare your husband's feelings."

"It was cowardice, not consideration for Joel, that made me implore you not to let the papers say much about me. I knew how his cold sarcasm would lash me if he ever found out I was still seeing Shirley."

"That was the whole root of your shrinking from notoriety?"

"In the beginning, yes. Joel hates my cousin and—judges her most harshly. I told you he'd forbidden my even seeing her. Afterward I had other reasons to fear his anger."

"You'd better give them to us," Fisk advised.

"Yes. Perhaps it was foolish to try and hide things." Fay spoke more confidently, rather as if the decision had already eased her. "You know I went to see Howard Munday immediately after the newspapers told about his daughter's death. I pretended it was the accounts of his poverty and broken health that had stirred my pity, but it wasn't only that. Three years ago, when Howard Munday was so horribly smashed in a motor accident, he appealed to my husband for help saying he'd recently lost his entire fortune in the stock market and was completely without funds. They must have known each other rather intimately a long time ago, judging by the letter which I opened and read by mistake. The letter made Joel furious, he wouldn't tell me why, and he refused to let me answer it or send the Mundays any money. I never heard of them again until after Nora was dead. Then I stupidly begged Joel to help the poor bedridden father who had once been his friend, and the former scene was repeated. He seemed so very angry that I didn't dare let him know I was secretly giving Howard Munday's landlady money for his board and care, so when I ran short of actual cash—Joel never lets me handle a great deal of it—I sold a ruby to Hilary Thorp, whom I'd heard was always willing to pay a fair price for a really good stone. Of course the money was for Howard Munday."

Her story seemed to interest Sydney Traherne much more deeply than it did the inspector. His lips were open to put some question when a second thought restrained the impulse and a queer veiled look wiped all expression from his face. Dr. Munro, who happened to be watching him, wondered what it was about Fay's apparently straightforward narrative that had so caught the playwright's interest, but being himself only an onlooker with no legitimate standing in the inquiry, he dared not ask. Whatever it was the point seemed to have escaped Conway Fisk; he accepted the story without comment, passing from it to the present afternoon.

"Does your husband object to your friendship with Mrs. Palmer?"

"Oh, no! Joel approves of her, indeed I think he likes her as much as he ever likes anybody."

"Had you any special reason for coming to-day?"

"No, of course not."

"You'd been here about how long, before you noticed Mr. Palmer's car standing outside?"

"Perhaps an hour, or a little less."

"And where were you before that?"

"Shopping. I also lunched downtown."

"Now, the lavender car wasn't in sight when you arrived?"

"Certainly not. My taxi stopped only a little way from where it was afterward parked."

"At least that narrows the time when the car turned up here down to the hour between three and four," Fisk reflected aloud. "At what time did you lunch, Mrs. Palmer?"

"We're very unfashionable and like an early luncheon; my husband left home a few minutes after one o'clock."

"That leaves two hours unaccounted for. Luckily the coupé's a very distinctive color, it's possible we can find some one who saw it between one and three."

As he finished speaking Constance Palmer uttered a sudden plaintive little moan, covering both ears with defensive hands; from the hall had come a sound of feet moving with the measured shuffle of men bearing a heavy burden.

"The medical examiner's here." Signing the doctor to stay with the two women Fisk beckoned Traherne and they both went out into the hall, where a policeman and the medical examiner's assistant were carrying the body of Lloyd Palmer toward the stairs leading up to his own room. At the stairhead James, the footman, hovered ready to show them the way, while from a corner the maidservant watched, her eyes big with awe.

"Pretty serious, inspector," the medical examiner remarked on a note of grave commiseration. "This makes four victims of the Perfumed Death."

"We can all imagine the howl due to go up from every newspaper in the country," Fisk gloomily agreed. "Unless I can soon show results I'm likely to be forced into resigning."

"Surely it's not that bad?" his friend protested.

"Worse, if anything. Naturally public and press object to seeing one harmless citizen after another struck down with apparently nothing done toward catching the murderer. Yet as a cold fact I've never in my life worked harder on a case."

"I suppose if we doctors could agree as to exactly how the poison's administered it would help a lot?"

"More, if you could tell me how long the infernal stuff takes to act. As it is I've no means of knowing what length of time elapses between the poison's introduction into a healthy system and the death that's apparently sure to follow. As a result it's impossible to eliminate any suspect because they've an alibi covering the fatal hour, since we don't know if it takes one or ten, or any other number of hours for the poison to kill. All that it's safe to conclude is that its effect is moderately slow, since both Nora Munday and Lloyd Palmer died while quite alone, and Cyril Kenwick was stricken half an hour after returning home."

"I can see the uncertainty concerning time must complicate matters," the medical examiner sympathized. "Let's hope we'll discover more about the poison through this last death than the former ones. I'd better go up and start examining Lloyd Palmer's body without further delay."

The footman had come downstairs after showing the way to his dead master's bedroom, but instead of offering to perform a similar service for the medical examiner he hung back, signing the maid to assume that duty, then, as soon as Traherne and the inspector were alone, his discreet cough announced that, while rigid training forbade his interrupting their low-toned conversation, he would be glad of an opportunity to unburden his mind.

"You've something to tell us, James?" The inspector's memory for names was only slightly inferior to his memory for faces.

"I don't know if it's important, sir." The footman came closer, his already lowered voice sinking a note or two as he added: "But when I first went out to Mr. Palmer there was no queer smell on his lips."

15

"Say that again!" The inspector caught James' arm, unconsciously shaking him in the stress of his sudden excitement.

"When Mrs. Palmer sent me to see was anything wrong I only thought Mr. Lloyd had drunk too much, but once I'd a good look at his face I knew he was dead—I leaned close enough to smell at his lips and there wasn't any scent on them."

"You're certain of that?"

"Oh, yes, sir. I leaned quite close."

"Why'd you do that?"

"Well, you see, sir, we've all been reading a lot about the people who die or get found dead, with a queer scent about their mouths—so I wondered if Mr. Palmer was another one."

"Then we've been classing him as a fourth victim of the Perfumed Death when he's nothing of the sort!" Fisk almost laughed in the greatness of his relief. "Shows how the unexplained can terrorize a group of sensible people! We're all so upset over the work of this mysterious poisoner that we simply take it for granted he's to blame for a new death without properly verifying the assumption."

"But—but—" James gulped distressfully, "the odd smell's on his lips now, sir, I couldn't but notice it upstairs when they carried him close by me through the door!"

For a second the inspector stared at him, while the significance of the statement slowly filtered into his slightly dazed brain. "You mean the scent's been added since you first found Lloyd Palmer's body?" Fisk found it hard to credit the man's story.

"It must have been, sir." James was very respectful but very certain of his facts.

"Then—let's try and get this straight; after you'd smelled Palmer's lips did you leave the body alone while you came back into the house?"

"I didn't come back, sir, at least not then," James asserted. "The ladies were watching from the window and must have guessed the trouble was serious for they both came out while I was still at the car window."

"Yes, go on," Fisk prompted as the footman betrayed a certain hesitation.

"Well, it was only Mrs. Redmond who leaned in through the window, sir, Mrs. Palmer didn't even go real close to the car."

"Hm-m." Though the idea was not actually put into words both men evidently suspected Fay of having perfumed Lloyd Palmer's dead lips. "You stayed near the body while the maid brought a policeman from his regular beat?"

"Yes, sir."

"And no one but Mrs. Redmond approached it?"

"No one. The ladies came back into the house and I followed as soon as the policeman came to relieve me."

"Just a second, Fisk." It was the first time Sydney Traherne had spoken since the utterance of James' startling announcement. "Before you accuse Fay of adding the scent remember that some time elapsed between James' re-entry into the house and our own arrival here. The body may have been tampered with during that interval."

"The police were guarding it."

"Even so, you'd better question them before assuming that nobody else went near the car. It might also be a good idea to test James' olfactory powers; he may have simply failed to detect it."

"Oh, I couldn't do that, sir," James was driven to protest. "It's a very strong smell, sir, very strong, indeed!"

"How plainly did you notice it yourself, Fisk?"

At the question a blank look overspread the inspector's face. "Why—I didn't notice it at all! I supposed it was because I've a head cold and can't smell properly."

"Do you mean to say you simply took it for granted Lloyd Palmer was another victim of this Perfumed Death, without in any way testing the supposition?" Traherne reproachfully demanded.

"Not ten minutes before I got word of his death you warned me he was in danger," the inspector defended his own credulous attitude. "Naturally Fay Redmond's message led me to believe our unknown poisoner had struck again—precisely as you'd foretold. Then, when we got here and found Lloyd Palmer's face wearing exactly the same agonized expression as Cyril Kenwick's, Nora Munday's, and Duncan's, and the same type of rubber band wrapped round his finger, it never occurred to me to doubt the conclusion. As I say, I thought my failure to detect the familiar odor was due to this cold in my head." Then, suddenly carrying the attack into the opposition camp, "It's a pity you didn't do a little smelling yourself, instead of waiting until now and jumping all over *me?*"

"There's something in what you say." Traherne smiled at his irate friend. "Want me to go have a talk with the policeman guarding the mauve coupé, while you finish cross examining the household?"

"Yes, and be sure to pin him down about the time between our coming inside and the medical examiner's arrival, as well as the earlier interval, though I'm willing to bet you'll find Fay is the only person who went near the body."

When Traherne had gone out to the policeman Fisk did his best to shake James' certainty as to the lack of any perfume when he first discovered Lloyd Palmer's body and failing, insisted on being taken to the kitchen where, with the help of various spices and condiments supplied by a heartily interested cook, he conducted several tests of James' sense of smell—finding it quite as efficient as that of the aforesaid cook, or the maidservant whose nose was also pressed into service.

That point settled to his satisfaction the inspector started for the room where he had left Mrs. Palmer and Fay in Dr. Munro's care, meaning to instantly call Fay to an accounting, but as he passed through the front hall Traherne entered it, closely followed by Zoe Panza. The sight of her alert, pleasantly expectant little face within the forbidden portals proved too much for the inspector's over-tried patience; he advanced, looking very much as if he meant to forcibly eject her.

"I thought I told you to stay outside?"

"Don't bite me, inspector dear, I'm under Mr. Traherne's wing." Zoe snuggled confidingly against Traherne's elbow, favoring the glowering inspector with a defiant glimpse of her pointed pink tongue.

"I brought her in because she's something to tell you, Fisk." Traherne spoke so gravely that his friend's manner instantly lost all belligerence.

"What is it?" His tone held only the impersonal attention due any witness who had evidence to impart and Zoe responded with an answering gravity.

"I went to the Dancing Bat this afternoon for a conference with Slithers. Lloyd Palmer was there, drinking like a fish, and he wasn't alone."

"Well go on, who was with him?"

"Jerome Tabour."

"Great Caesar! Tabour—!" The little gray cells in Fisk's head felt as if they were suddenly doing an inspired can-can. "Are you sure?"

"Of course I'm sure. Wasn't I formally introduced to Jerome Tabour only last night? And I've known both the Palmer twins for years."

"What time did you see them?"

"Somewhere around two o'clock. The manager or waiter can probably verify the time if it's important."

Jerome Tabour! If she was right, and the inspector knew Zoe Panza too well to entertain much doubt as to the accuracy of any information supplied by her, it meant that Shirley Tabour's ex-husband entered into three out of the four murders included in his investigation. At the time of Cyril Kenwick's death Jerome Tabour's possible guilt had been considered, mainly because no one else seemed to possess the faintest reason for desiring the lad's removal and Tabour might, just conceivably, be credited with jealousy of Cyril's success with his own former wife. But under the circumstances the motive had appeared too inadequate to justify serious suspicion.

Even when he was found to be the only person admittedly near the second poison victim, Nora Munday, within several hours of her death, he was again saved by lack of a convincing motive. His third entry into the case, however, rather changed the aspect of his association with the two earlier victims; Inspector Fisk began to doubt if coincidence could be held responsible for Tabour's triple appearance and to regretfully wonder if some connection between him and old Hilary Thorp had not been overlooked in the heat of Gentsy Judd's pursuit. As if in answer to his thought Zoe Panza unexpectedly supplied the missing fourth link.

"I told you I met Jerome Tabour socially, last night. It was at his ex-wife's apartment where I'd called to get an interview with Shirley for my paper. He wasn't there all the time and after he'd gone I loudly admired a huge black opal Shirley was wearing set in a ring. She told me Jerome Tabour had just given it to her as a kind of second engagement ring—of course you know they're planning to remarry. Well, while playing maid in the Thorp house I rather made friends with Duncan, who wasn't half such a dour person as Teddy makes out, in fact he was quite susceptible to a little judicious flattery, and while I dusted the jewel room Saturday afternoon he so far unbent that he showed me half a dozen very special stones he was polishing—one of them is the big black opal set in Shirley's new ring."

"Careful," Fisk warned. "Don't let your flair for a good story carry you away. All Hilary Thorp's jewels were unset and unless you're an expert it isn't easy to tell one stone from another when you've no setting to help the identification."

"Quite true—with the majority of jewels," Zoe conceded. "This black opal is different; in its heart there's a splash of brilliant green flame forming an almost perfect cross. I doubt if the most flagrant amateur could fail to recognize it."

"And you say Tabour only gave it to his wife last night." The inspector had evidently accepted Zoe's identification of the black opal as final. "That gives plenty of time since the robbery to have the opal set in a ring. Of course you realize that what you tell us brings Tabour in touch with all four murders, since you saw him at the Dancing Bat with Lloyd Palmer. The Dancing Bat—" He abruptly checked himself, he had just remembered seeing Jerome and Shirley Tabour enter the club only a few nights ago, practically in the wake of the Palmer twins. "Zoe, you're forgiven for forcing a way in here, your news amply earns an entry. Why the dickens didn't you give it to me outside?"

"Much chance I had, when you almost bit me for trying to speak!" she reproached him. "Please, inspector dear, may my paper tell its readers to watch for the coming arrest of a wealthy and popular New Yorker?"

"Print one word of what you've told us to-day and I'll gently but firmly slaughter you," the inspector warned. "Above all things I want to avoid letting Tabour know he's suspected until we've had time to thoroughly investigate his past life and, let's hope, unearthed his motive for such a coldblooded series of crimes. At the present showing we've not nearly enough evidence against him to face a jury trial with any real hope of a conviction."

"Maybe I can help delve into his scarlet past," Zoe hopefully suggested.

"No. If you really want to be useful cultivate Shirley Tabour—there's an even chance that she knows more than she's told."

"Right." The girl's sunny smile thanked him for delegating so congenial a task. "By now Teddy's probably tired of waiting for me, and taking him along gives an excuse for dropping in on Shirley's popular cocktail hour; I'll bet she never refuses welcome to a nice mannered boy."

When she had flashed out through the front door Traherne unkindly put a question that pricked the bubble of his friend's swelling satisfaction.

"How about the absence of perfume on Palmer's lips when his body was first found? Jerome Tabour had no chance to add it."

"Hell!" The word was low voiced but filled with sincere disgust. "And there's not an earthly thing the matter with James' sense of smell—I've been putting it through its paces in the kitchen!" Then, with a sudden gleam of restored confidence: "Most likely we were wrong in thinking any one had doctored Palmer's lips—probably the perfume isn't noticeable until the victim has been dead for some little time."

"That's a possible explanation," Traherne admitted. "There's another question I wanted to ask; did you notice how much Constance Palmer disliked talking about what her husband had for lunch?"

"Probably worrying for fear she'll be accused of setting an indigestible table. I doubt if the idea of murder has occurred to her." Fisk dismissed the matter as unimportant. "Of course whatever food or drink he took to-day will have to be examined, but it's hardly more than routine work. Zoe's news makes it pretty clear Jerome Tabour is the one we've got to concentrate on."

"Wasn't Tabour investigated at the time of young Kenwick's death?"

"Yes, but not half as thoroughly as he's going to be investigated within the next few days. Before I finish we'll know more about Tabour's past life than he does himself. Care to work with me, or have you lines of your own that need following?"

"Several. I'll keep in touch with you by phone. And, for the Lord's sake give me advance notice before you arrest Jerome Tabour."

Pursuing one of the several lines he had mentioned, Traherne visited the Dancing Bat that night in search of the stool-pigeon known as Slithers. The police had released the little gambler when repeated cross questioning failed to shake his story of the Thorp robbery in the smallest degree, and Traherne knew the Dancing Bat was one of his favorite haunts.

He was fortunate enough to find Slithers in one of the club's inner rooms, where, for a certain generous remuneration, he consented to again repeat his often-told story and answer a few additional questions from Traherne, whom he knew as Conway Fisk's friend and unofficial co-adjutor.

It was only when Traherne mentioned his desire for a talk with Gentsy Judd's sweetheart, Trixie, that Slithers actually balked, flatly refusing to arrange a meeting. Threats of police pressure failing to move him, Traherne gave it up and finally procured an introduction to the girl through the Dancing Bat's manager instead.

Trixie's attitude was distrustful and discouragingly close-mouthed, the utmost concession Traherne could win being a promise to transmit a brief message to Gentsy Judd, who she insisted was still in Montreal.

16

"It's horrible to blame me for Lloyd's death when I loved him with all my heart!"

"My dear Mrs. Palmer, I've tried to explain that I'm doing nothing of the sort." Traherne, watching her helplessly dab at persistently streaming eyes felt a strong inclination to shake her; he hated flaccid inefficiency in man or woman.

"But you did! You asked what I was hiding about Lloyd's luncheon!"

"Only because I reasoned that, loving your husband as you say you did, you would naturally want to help us catch and punish his murderer," he patiently went on explaining. "Of course I realize you would never have willingly harmed Mr. Palmer—but I also realize you weren't altogether frank about that last meal of his and I want you to trust me enough to tell what it is you're keeping back."

"Nothing, nothing at all!" she protested a trifle too vehemently.

"There is something," Traherne placidly insisted. "I was watching yesterday when Inspector Fisk first questioned you. There was some fact which you failed to tell." He waited, in the faint hope of a voluntary statement, and when none was forthcoming leaned a little closer, his oddly striped eyes fixed unescapably on her tear-streaked face. "You probably think me a brute for hammering you with questions, but there's no time for squeamishness—the mysterious poisoner who strikes with the most cowardly of all weapons, must be caught!"

"I can't see why you should come to me for assistance—it's very cruel of you."

"Cruel perhaps, but necessary, because I think you've been used as a tool."

"Oh!" Horror almost dried her tears at their source. "Oh! How terrible! Surely you can't mean that."

"Not a willing or even a conscious tool," Traherne hastened to qualify his statement. "Nevertheless I suspect that in some way you've been tricked into executing his design. Be frank with me, Mrs. Palmer, tell me what you've been hiding."

"If you are right—if what I did was really the cause of Lloyd's death, I shall never forgive myself—never!"

"It would be much more to the point if you tried to atone for whatever it was you did, by helping us get on the poisoner's track," Traherne rather dryly pointed out.

"I'm becoming terribly afraid you may be right, though heaven knows I only meant to help Lloyd, not harm him."

"That I quite understand. Now tell me what it was you did."

"People constantly do the same sort of thing," Constance Palmer weakly excused what she was about to tell. "The magazines and newspapers are full of advertisements showing how devoted wives give their husbands medicine guaranteed to kill the longing for strong drink!"

"So *that* was it." Light was beginning to dawn. "Go on, tell me exactly what happened."

"Well, of course you know how Lloyd and his brother drank, not sometimes but all the time. It's been growing worse and worse every year, and since they retired from business they've practically never been sober. Perhaps you can imagine, a little, what it has meant to me! I did everything I could think of to make Lloyd stop, but it was perfectly useless, he never paid the slightest attention. Then, about six months ago, an Indian herb doctor wrote me saying he knew my husband was a victim of alcoholism and suggesting that I let him try to cure the disease, for he said after a certain stage was reached the craving for alcohol became an actual sickness. This herb doctor went on to explain how easily one of the antidotes for alcoholism could be slipped into Lloyd's coffee without his ever knowing, but to me it seemed unfair to cure him like that, without his own consent, so I did nothing about it."

"You saved the letter?" Traherne's anxiety drove him into demanding.

"No, not that one. I threw it away after only a casual reading. Another one came a few weeks later, but I didn't save that either. Then, just a week ago I received a third and that one I kept because Lloyd and Bronson had been drinking so heavily that I felt unless something was done to stop them they'd both surely die. Truly I didn't act without giving the matter a great deal of thought, I even sounded Lloyd, very discreetly, to discover if he would willingly try the herb doctor's cure—he was so disagreeable that I dared not press the subject; instead I let the doctor know on Thursday, that I wanted his antidote for alcoholism."

She hesitated an instant, then gathered courage to plunge into full confession.

"He sent it next day, yesterday, and at luncheon Lloyd complained of a frightful headache, saying he must have eaten something that disagreed with him, so, when luncheon was over I persuaded him to take the herb doctor's remedy, telling him it was for indigestion!"

She stopped, her eyes hungrily begging for reassurance.

"Surely that one pill couldn't—couldn't *kill* Lloyd?"

"I'm afraid that's exactly what it did." Traherne felt it more merciful to end her suspense. Then before realization drove her to a fresh outburst of grief, he asked for the herb doctor's third letter.

"But I haven't it!" Mrs. Palmer sobbed. "I destroyed it as soon as Lloyd had taken the pill, for fear he might learn what I'd done."

If vocally expressed Traherne's feelings would have turned the air blue. "At least you remember the herb doctor's name and address?" he suggested in a voice carefully purged of all expression.

"I do remember his name, it was Dr. Salmon, but I never knew his address."

"Yet I understood you to say you wrote for this medicine."

"Not quite that. I said I let him know I wanted it," Constance Palmer corrected.

"How could you do that if you hadn't his address?"

"Why, in all his letters he told me how he traveled through the rural districts in a caravan, selling his medicines to the country people. If I wanted him to cure my husband I was to let him know by inserting a notice in the personal column of a certain daily paper—that's what I did, of course, and as I tell you the medicine came next day."

"It didn't strike you as singular that he could send it so quickly when he was supposed to be traveling through the country?"

"Why—no, though I see now it couldn't have reached me so soon if he'd been telling the truth."

"Precisely how was the notice in the personal column to read?"

"Let me think, I'm sure I can remember it in a moment, yes—'Constance needs help for a loved one, please send at once.'"

"Nothing else?"

"Nothing."

"Now, please describe this 'pill' I think you called it."

She did so, Traherne listening with the utmost attention.

"So? And he was to swallow it washed down with a little water?"

"Yes."

"Did you burn, or simply tear up the herb doctor's last letter?"

"I burned it," she regretfully confessed. "Oh!" with a sudden flash of recollection: "Would the envelope help at all?"

"It might. Didn't you destroy that along with the letter?"

"No. It was such heavy paper and the letter itself took so long to burn that I didn't bother burning the envelope; besides it couldn't have told Lloyd about the cure even if he'd happened to find it. Please wait while I run up to my room and see if it's still there."

She returned with it in her hand much sooner than Traherne had dared to hope. Casually looked at the plain white envelope had very little to tell, hardly more than the hour of mailing and the Post Office Station, for there was no return address of any kind. Still it was better than nothing and might prove more communicative when examined under a microscope; carefully folding it in a handkerchief to avoid destroying finger prints or other possible clews he put it in an inner pocket, then inquired about the wrapper or box in which the single pill was sent. Mrs. Palmer, after a little thought, remembered having thrown it into the fire which an unseasonably chilly morning had made welcome at breakfast time; the hour when the fatal pill arrived.

After a few more questions Traherne thanked her and said good-by. He was crossing the hall on his way out when the footman, James, coming quickly down the stairs intercepted him.

"Beg pardon, sir, but could you spare a few minutes for Mr. Bronson? He's not well enough to leave his room, sir, but most anxious to see you."

Traherne's single meeting with the surviving Palmer brother had not been of a nature to breed desire for a second, still the man might have something to tell so he let James show the way to his room.

Bronson Palmer appeared to have aged a score of years in the last twenty-four hours. He was huddled in an armchair by the window, his bright silk dressing gown accentuating the shriveled, leathery look of a skin so shrunken that the bony structure of his face threatened to indecently pierce its scanty covering.

"Have you caught him? Do you know who did it?" The old man's eagerness ignored the amenities of ordinary greeting.

"Not yet. We've had very little time, you know." Traherne sat down, regarding the other with critical and none too friendly eyes; he was not a pleasant looking old gentleman.

"James tells me you're helping the police inspector. Can't the two of you find out who killed Lloyd?"

"You seem to forget it's not the first crime of its kind, but one of a series. We have yet to discover some one with a reason for wanting all four victims removed. Perhaps you can help us by telling of any one, man or woman, who hated your brother."

"Lots of people did, lots of 'em." The old gentleman emitted a kind of croaking chuckle. "Lloyd wasn't soft-handed in the way of business, he made plenty of enemies, and as for the women! Well, they haven't interested him these last few years, but up to then he gave a good few reason for cursing him."

"Must have been a nice, honorable type!" was Traherne's expressionless comment.

"Honorable? Of course he was honorable!" Bronson Palmer peered at him suspiciously from under deeply wrinkled lids that half hid the evil old eyes. "If he got the best of fools, male or female, there's no law against that, is there?"

"Perhaps not, but knowing he was so generally hated doesn't help us to locate his murderer," Traherne pointed out. "You can't think of any specific enemy who'd vowed vengeance?"

"No-o, or at least not lately," the old man decided after a little reflection. "Of course when we got out of business Lloyd stopped tramping on so many people's pet corns, and as for the ladies—they ceased to matter quite some years ago."

"This business that you mention, what was it?"

"We were tea importers, on a large scale."

"Nothing more harmful than tea?"

"He-he—" Palmer's leer and cackling giggle told of contraband opium as plainly as a spoken admission. "But there was never any trouble with the Government," he carefully explained. "Too respectable a firm ever to be suspected."

"A long-established firm?" There was a slightly anxious note in Traherne's voice, as if a good deal depended on the answer.

"Oh, no! Lloyd liked trying different lines, he'd been in several, all of them profitable, before we started the tea business."

"I think Mrs. Palmer mentioned that Joel Redmond was associated with you and your brother?"

"That's truer than most of Constance's facts, and speaking confidentially, he was one of the reasons why we quit. Neither of us could get on with him, sour, pessimistic old swine, it's an outrage for him to have such a pretty wife!"

Traherne passed the reference to Fay without comment, sticking closely to the business issue.

"Did Joel Redmond carry on alone?"

"No, the business was dissolved; he went into factories."

"But friendly relations continued? There was no trouble between you?"

"Oh, no. Joel was scared and more anxious to give up the—tea—business than we were. Everything worked smooth as silk. See here—" The old man leaned forward, an outstretched hand on Traherne's knee. "All this talk about business leads us nowhere—I want Lloyd's murderer caught!"

"That's a desire we hold in common—more, I intend to see that he, or she, is caught and punished."

"I'll make it worth your while, damned if I won't! My brother was the one thing on earth I cared about—without him I'd as soon be dead, sooner, for then I either wouldn't know I was lonely or I'd have plenty of spicy friends. Catch his murderer and—would the promise of twenty thousand be any inducement?"

"Not the slightest. I'm not in this case for what I can get out of it, I'm simply after the killer, and—if it's any comfort to you I don't mind saying the trail is getting fairly warm."

17

"There's a Dr. Alan Munro outside who insists on seeing you, inspector."

"What does he want?" The inspector looked up from a gloomy perusal of the latest virulent attack on himself and the police force in general; the press was becoming almost hysterical over the continued lack of arrests in what was termed The Perfumed Death Inquiry.

"He won't say, except that it's important."

"Better bring him in," Fisk directed, more or less glad of an excuse for laying aside the paper.

"Sorry to disturb you so early." Dr. Munro's face looked curiously haggard in the strong morning light. "But I'm in trouble—Fay Redmond is missing!"

"Now, precisely what do you mean by 'missing'?" The inspector felt distinctly aggrieved; matters were already bad enough without the added infliction of a vanished woman and one, at that, so closely connected with the case he was on as to make it impossible to pass the search for her over to the Bureau of Missing Persons. "Has she failed to keep an appointment with you, or disappeared from her home?"

"Both!" The doctor's acute anxiety was almost indecently apparent. "Her husband was to have gone out of town yesterday and we arranged to dine and spend the evening together." He broke off at sight of Fisk's quizzical eyebrows. "For God's sake don't misunderstand our friendship, don't class Fay in the same category as her cousin!" he besought. "She has the misfortune to be married to a man anything but kind to her—the friendship which has sprung up between us is no more than that, a friendship that brings a little sunlight into her restricted life."

"Oh, I quite understand." The inspector nodded sympathetically. "It's nothing warmer than platonic affection that makes you look the ghost of your normal self—because the lovely Fay failed to keep an appointment."

"It's not only that. I tell you she's completely disappeared!"

"So far you've told me nothing of the kind," Fisk retorted. "Been too busy white-washing your intimacy with a married woman. If you want my help you'd better start at the beginning and tell me exactly what *has* happened."

"As I tell you, we had a dinner appointment last night. I waited almost two hours but Fay never came. I dared not call her home, fearing Joel Redmond had postponed leaving town and that was why she couldn't get away. The disappointment and uncertainty kept me from sleeping and in the night I remembered Fay's telling me her husband's business trip was particularly important so there would be no doubt about his going. After that memory returned to me I grew terribly anxious, so much so that I called her house this morning—the maid who answered told me Mrs. Redmond hadn't been home all night!"

"Probably with Shirley Tabour or some other woman friend," Fisk interjected as the doctor paused.

"Perhaps, but her servants are alarmed about her."

"You've talked to them?"

"Yes. After phoning Shirley Tabour and Mrs. Palmer—the only friends of Fay's I know—I went up to the Redmond house."

"Humph, taking a good deal on yourself, weren't you? The visit may be hard for her to explain."

"I had to know," the doctor defended his own impulsive behavior. "Don't you realize that Fay wouldn't disappoint me without serious cause?"

"Such close friends as that, are you? Well, what have her servants to say?"

"They are worried, but hardly know what to do. It seems this isn't the first time she's unexpectedly stayed away over night when her husband was out of town, but she's always let them know either by phoning, or sending a wire. That's what they thought had happened last night—that she'd sent a wire which was in some way delayed. When none came this morning they began getting really frightened. If I hadn't taken charge they'd have notified the police on their own account."

"What time yesterday did Fay leave home?"

"Not long after lunch. She was driven down town, made several purchases at various shops, then left the car on 35th street while she went into Altman's, telling her chauffeur she might be gone some little time as she had a number of errands to do. The man waited almost two hours, then when she still hadn't come back, he went into the store to try and find her, wandering aimlessly about but seeing nothing of Mrs. Redmond. Finally he asked the doorman at one of the entrances whether he had heard of any customer taken suddenly ill, and was told that nothing of the kind had happened that day, so far as the doorman knew. Thinking Mrs. Redmond might have forgotten just where the car was parked and failing to find it, gone home in a taxi, the chauffeur telephoned to the house but found nothing had been heard of her there. Not knowing what else to do he waited until closing time, then drove home. All evening they expected a message from Fay and when none came either last night or this morning one of them sent a wire to the hotel address in Albany left by Joel Redmond; that was before I got to the house?"

"Has he answered?"

"He hadn't up to half an hour ago."

"H-m-m." Fisk was mentally reviewing the doctor's story. "So Fay went into Altman's store yesterday afternoon and as far as her chauffeur knows, never came out again. If I'm not mistaken Altman's covers an entire block with doors on all four sides; an excellently chosen spot from which to disappear."

"That sounds as though you thought Fay had vanished of her own accord!"

"Use your common sense, man. She surely couldn't have been forcibly kidnaped in a crowded department store."

"It's equally impossible to imagine her voluntarily entering Altman's by one door and leaving it by another, when she knew her car was waiting!"

"Think so? Yet it's an ideal method of dropping out of sight. With so many exits, through all of which women of her own class were constantly passing, the task of picking up Fay's trail looks pretty hopeless."

"Do you mean you intend making no effort to find her?"

"Oh, quite the contrary—the fact that she was frightened badly enough to take to her heels doubles my interest in the lady. Prejudice aside, doctor, you'll have to admit that people don't walk off like that unless they've good reason to be scared. Fay must have guessed how closely we've linked her with the Perfumed Death."

"That's sheer nonsense—insane twaddle!" Dr. Munro jumped up to pace restlessly about the office. "Of *course* Fay has no reason to be afraid. I tell you she's either been kidnaped or—killed!"

"Under the eyes of fifty salesclerks and as many customers?" the inspector sarcastically inquired. "Don't be an idiot."

"She must have been lured into some less public place; perhaps by a forged message from me."

"This grows serious; so you feel sure a message, supposedly from you, could easily inveigle Mrs. Redmond into visiting some secluded place where she could be conveniently kidnaped, or otherwise disposed of—granting, of course, that somebody has a reason for wanting her out of the way."

"She'd have no earthly reason for distrusting a message which she thought came from me." Dr. Munro's tone sounded rather sulky; he seemed to resent the inspector's whole attitude. "It would be more to the point if, instead of sitting there making insinuations against Fay Redmond, you tried to find out what's become of her. Personally I believe she's fallen victim to this mysterious poisoner who's clever enough to laugh at the entire police force."

"The laugh will be on the other side before we reach the end," Fisk quietly promised.

"If so, won't it be largely due to Sydney Traherne's efforts?" There was the faintest edge of a sneer in Dr. Munro's voice, but the inspector was too loyal an admirer of Traherne to in the least resent it.

"Quite possibly—and what's more it won't be the first time he's saved us from failure. He's an uncanny faculty for picking the essential clew in any inquiry and following it regardless of all minor issues."

"Why not get in touch with him now? I'd feel safer with him on Fay's trail."

"Nothing I'd like better, but I don't know where Traherne is; he's not at his apartment and his man claims to have no idea where he's gone or when he'll return. In his absence you'll have to leave the search for Fay in our hands." He paused, adding rather grimly: "While I admit hating to furnish the press with more fuel for the bonfire that's cremating the Force's reputation, it's got to be done;

publicity gives the best hope of finding Fay and we'll need an accurate description of what she was wearing yesterday. Did you think to ask the chauffeur?"

"No. The idea of broadcasting her description never occurred to me. She will intensely dislike such notoriety."

"Can't be helped. Fay is beautiful enough to attract attention, some fellow shopper may have seen her in Altman's and noticed by which door she left, or—well, there's never any telling just what results publishing the description of a missing person may bring."

In this particular instance it brought none of the slightest value. Any number of people insisted they had seen the missing woman at points as far apart as Newark and the Bronx, but investigation proved such reports lacked a solid foundation. In Altman's itself two or three clerks who were in the habit of waiting on Fay Redmond remembered selling her various articles, and in the millinery department the police learned she had bought a hat, leaving the old one to be sent home while she wore the new. This latter fact, Inspector Fisk considered, suggested a wish to alter her appearance and so bore out his contention of a voluntary flight, but voluntarily or otherwise, Fay had certainly vanished with a completeness that defied all efforts to trace her.

On learning that his wife was missing Joel Redmond abandoned his business trip, returning to New York where he made the inspector's life additionally unpleasant by haunting police headquarters and giving unbridled rein to a wrathful and sarcastic tongue.

Shirley Tabour's hysterical grief over what she told several interested reporters she felt convinced was her cousin's murder, further added to Fisk's woes, so that by the time Sydney Traherne telephoned him on the second day after Fay's disappearance he had reached a distinctly snappish frame of mind.

"Hope you've been enjoying your holiday," was his first remark after recognizing Traherne's voice. "I was beginning to think you'd eloped with Fay Redmond."

"Nice of you, I'm sure, considering how I've been slaving in your interests." Traherne's voice sounded annoyingly cheerful. "Anything been heard of her, by the way?"

"Not a whisper. At first I thought she feared implication in the poison murders enough to have taken to her heels—now I'm getting to the point where I expect somebody to report discovering her dead body with that accursed perfume clinging to its lips."

Traherne ignored the gloomy prognostication. "You've made no move against Jerome Tabour?"

"None, though I've put in my spare time dissecting his hectic past, he seems—"

"Don't give me your findings now," his friend hurriedly interposed. "There's a chance of some one listening in. Can you meet me in about an hour? I've certain plans that want talking over."

They arranged to lunch together at a favorite chophouse, and once Conway Fisk was off the wire Traherne called the newspaper which employed Zoe Panza. Failing to find her there he tried the Thorp house and was told by the housekeeper that Miss Panza had taken young Teddy Thorp to luncheon at Shirley Tabour's apartment. Finally catching her there he gave his name, then asked if Zoe had an engagement for that evening.

"Nothing that can't be put off if there's something getting ready to break," was her instant response.

"There is," he assured her, "and knowing how interested you are in the Perfumed Death Case I thought I'd pass you the tip. You've doubtless heard that suspicion points to Jerome Tabour as the killer—I'm not saying he'll be arrested to-night but—be at Howard Munday's boarding place at nine, we're expecting some interesting developments."

18

"Sure the excitement won't prove too much for you, Mr. Munday?"

"Positive." The old man's leonine head nodded with a certain grim emphasis. "Nora's death has left me with only one strong desire in life—to see her murderer punished. Since Mohammed cannot go to the mountain it is most kind of you to bring the mountain—in the form of this final scene—to me."

"Not so much kindness, Mr. Munday, as because two witnesses can more easily testify here than elsewhere," Sydney Traherne quietly explained.

"It's after nine." Inspector Fisk turned from the window through which he had been anxiously watching the street, watch in hand. "I hope there'll be no slip-up."

"Give them a few minutes' grace." Sydney Traherne was much less perturbed than his friend; perhaps because the plan of campaign was entirely his and he felt no doubt of his own ability to carry it to a successful finish.

"Here's a car now." Fisk was again watching the street. "The devil—it's Zoe Panza but she's not alone, Teddy Thorp's with her."

"No matter, she won't let him come up," Traherne soothed. "And if I were you I'd sit down, you'll look less like a spider hungrily awaiting its prey."

With an obvious effort the inspector followed his advice, settling in one of the rickety chairs and occupying the hands that refused to stay quite idle with the lighting of a cigarette.

True to Traherne's prediction it was only Zoe Panza who entered when the landlady opened the door a moment or two later; she had prudently left her escort outside. The girl's dark eyes flashed over the room in search of Jerome Tabour, and not seeing him, homed on Sydney Traherne.

"*Please* don't tell me I'm to be disappointed of those developments," she begged.

"Our friend's a bit late but I imagine he'll be along presently. Fisk and I made it plain there'd be unpleasant consequences should he fail to keep the appointment. If you'll all excuse me a second I'll go tell the landlady we're expecting him."

In his absence Inspector Fisk introduced Zoe to Howard Munday, whom she had not hitherto met. The bedridden man was too preoccupied to pay her more than the scantest attention.

"I've kept an eye on your paper and been glad to see it hasn't dropped a hint about Jerome Tabour's probable guilt." The inspector offered Zoe a cigarette which she accepted just as Traherne silently reentered the room.

"Going to reward discretion by giving me some inside facts about Fay's disappearance?"

"There aren't any," was Fisk's discouraged answer. "Whoever selected the place and mode of her vanishing possessed positive genius—it's proved impossible to pick up the trail of one particular woman among so many of a similar class and type."

"Aren't the papers saying flattering things about you?" Zoe favored him with a curly-lipped, slightly impish grin. "Hope you've noticed with what comparative tenderness mine has handled your reputation?"

"If that's your idea of tenderness God deliver me from what you'd call a real hauling over the coals!"

"Here he comes." Sydney Traherne's abnormally acute ears had identified Tabour's sluggish steps mounting the stairs before the others realized there was any one approaching.

As he paused at the door left half open by Traherne, Jerome Tabour gave the effect of hating to enter. Even when he had nerved himself into facing what he must regard as something in the nature of an ordeal, his puffy-lidded eyes flickered with an imperfectly mastered fear which he tried to hide under a slightly blustering manner.

"Evening, Inspector, evening, Traherne, hello, Zoe—what're you doing in the slums?" Then, without waiting for an answer, he swung to directly address Conway Fisk. "Mind telling me why I've been dragged way down here?"

"We thought you might prefer a private session to one held at police headquarters," Fisk quietly explained. "This is Howard Munday, Mr. Tabour, I think you two haven't met before; though you appear to know Miss Panza."

"Of course I know her, isn't she a pal of my wife's?" Traherne silently noted that the girl must have acted on their advice and cultivated Shirley Tabour; also the dropping of that abysmal little prefix "ex."

"Now I've followed your rather peremptory instructions and turned up at a beastly inconvenient hour, I hope you'll make the meeting as brief as possible. I've an engagement."

"Sorry to disappoint you, but there's not much chance of your getting away under a couple of hours," Inspector Fisk discouragingly informed him. "It's become necessary to go back to the beginning of the inquiry into Cyril Kenwick's death and pick up several loose threads. Better sit down and make the best of it."

"Pity you didn't at least select a place containing decent chairs." Tabour cautiously lowered his bulk into a chair which received it with an ominously protesting creak. "And I can't see why I should be pestered over the death of a boy I never so much as saw."

"For one thing, I understand that after letting your ex-wife severely alone for a couple of years you suddenly began seeing a good deal of her, and showed decided jealousy over her engagement to Cyril Kenwick."

"Who's responsible for that yarn?" Tabour wanted to know. "It's true Shirley and I lunched together a few times, but it wasn't because we'd any special craving for each other's company—she was simply trying to make me settle some money on her in place of the alimony which I'd naturally quit paying once she married somebody else."

"That may account for the meetings," Fisk conceded. "How about the jealousy?"

"There wasn't any! Whoever told you I cared a hoop what Shirley did was lying."

"You and she never quarreled over Cyril Kenwick?"

"Certainly not." Then, with a sudden enlightenment, "If it was Shirley who handed you that bit of pure fiction she only did it to prove she hadn't lost her attraction for me. Don't you know women well enough to realize that a pretty one never admits a man who once loved her could possibly stop?"

"In this instance the lady seems to have been right. I've heard you and Shirley intend venturing a second wedding."

"That's a fact," the ex-husband admitted, "but it wouldn't have happened except that we were sort of drawn together by being mixed up in these murder cases; we've both discovered there's a certain comfortable safety about marriage."

"So, getting back to said murder cases, you deny showing any jealousy of Cyril Kenwick?"

"Of course I do, I hadn't any to show."

"And you don't admit knowing him, or being in Shirley's apartment during his last visit there?"

"The first time I ever went into the place was days after young Kenwick died. Mr. Traherne was there at the time, he can bear me out in saying Shirley was astonished when I unexpectedly blew in."

Traherne merely nodded an absentminded assent. "There's one question touching the Kenwick case that I've always wanted to ask." He turned toward Zoe Panza. "I wasn't there myself but the inspector told me how promptly you appeared on the scene. I'm puzzled over how you knew a murder had been committed."

"How I knew? Why, Inspector Fisk explains it by declaring there's some leak at headquarters."

"And you, yourself?"

"Oh, I make a point of never trying to explain anything—it's such a terrible waste of energy."

"You won't even tell us who let you into the Kenwick house?" Then, as she simply stared at him, he went smoothly on, apparently reflecting aloud. "No one admits having done so; I've questioned Barnabus, the inspector's plain clothes men, the medical examiner's assistants; in fact every one who was in the house that night. Nobody remembers having seen you enter. Queer. I've been tempted to wonder exactly how long you had been there before Inspector Fisk discovered you."

There was an odd little pause, broken by a sharp tattoo on the closed door.

"Come in," Traherne called so promptly that one might easily have imagined the knock expected.

A small boy whom none of the others had ever seen before marched gravely into the room, one chubby hand clutching a large white envelope.

"That's for me, I think." Sydney Traherne opened the letter and, with a murmured word of apology, glanced at its contents, then fished for a dime with which to reward the small messenger who had meanwhile stood, staring round-eyed from one to another.

"Here you are, son."

"Yes, sir, yes." The little fellow turned and marched solemnly out again.

The small episode appeared to have shut off the current of Traherne's curiosity, he relapsed into silence, leaving the inspector free to carry on his cross examination of Jerome Tabour.

"Next we'll take up the second murder of the series," he began. "As far as we can learn, Mr. Tabour, you told the truth about your first meeting with Nora Munday and the subsequent dinner engagement. But of course we're quite ignorant of what happened between you and the girl while you were alone together in your car. Looked at impartially it seems suspicious that after having been more or less connected with the first poison victim through your wife, you should have spent all those hours alone with the second victim just before her death."

"Yes, I can see that." Tabour's nervousness was becoming more and more obvious. "All the same you can't get round the fact that I'd no earthly motive in either case."

"None that has so far been announced," his questioner coldly corrected.

"Meaning that you think you've discovered one?" Tabour anxiously demanded.

"I haven't said so. As it happens we haven't yet reached the point where it's necessary to discuss motives. At present we're dealing only with facts. Now, in first recounting what occurred during the evening Nora Munday spent with you, you claimed to have been quite alone in the roadhouse near Tarrytown, except, of course, for the other diners. Is that accurate?"

"Certainly it is. I had no reason for lying."

"Quite sure you didn't even *see* any one you knew?"

"Not a soul."

"I ask because recent inquiries at the roadhouse have brought out the fact that a taxi bearing a solitary passenger stopped there almost immediately after you and Nora entered the roadhouse. At the time one of the attendants got an impression that the taxi was following your car. Whether that was true or not its passenger alighted and after paying and dismissing the taxi, went into the roadhouse where I thought you might possibly have seen her."

"Her?" Tabour repeated with a decidedly startled intonation. "Who was it? Shirley?"

"Why Shirley? I thought at that period you and the former Mrs. Tabour were supposed not to be interested in one another's movements."

"Well, we weren't, but I can't think of any other woman who was interested enough to follow me," Tabour sulkily declared. "Did the attendant describe her?"

"Yes. As an unusually small woman, or girl, he wasn't quite sure which, very dark and wearing tailor-made clothes."

"Humph, doesn't fit any little pet of mine, I'd always a preference for blondes. Could you find out what she did inside the roadhouse?"

"Nothing at all suspicious. Simply ordered a light meal, ate it, went into the ladies' dressing room (which I think you said Nora Munday also visited, by the way), and afterwards telephoned for another taxi in which she drove away from the roadhouse some little time before you did—if your memory of the hour at which you left is accurate, that is."

"I can't see any reason for hooking this unknown female up with me, or with Miss Munday," Tabour objected after a moment's consideration of the facts.

"No, except that after leaving the roadhouse she behaved rather oddly. She told the second taxi driver to take her down to the Tarrytown railroad station where she paid and dismissed him. He naturally supposed she meant taking a train and thought nothing more about her until some intensive inquiries in the Tarrytown vicinity brought her back to his mind. In the station itself no one seems to have noticed this girl, or woman, and the next we hear of her she is hiring a third taxi in the Tarrytown main street. This driver was told to go slowly along the Post road until she told him to stop—which she presently did at a spot he has since identified as no more than a couple of hundred yards from your roadhouse. There he was told to draw into the roadside as his passenger was feeling ill and the car's motion made her worse.

"They remained parked for some little time, during which a good many cars naturally passed. At last the unidentified lady declared herself well enough to go on and after that there was no question of driving slowly; she urged him along the Post road at a rattling pace until they neared Van Cortlandt Park, where he vaguely remembers seeing a stalled car. Very soon after passing it the lady told him to stop, as the car's motion was again making her sick. She said her destination was close by and she would go the rest of the way on foot, so paid him off and went on, walking very slowly. Turning, the man headed straight back for his home town, thereby immediately losing sight of his recent fare.

"Doesn't the whole procedure strongly suggest that the lady waited near the roadhouse until your car went by, followed it and when your breakdown occurred deserted her Tarrytown taxi?"

"But—Good God, why should she want to follow me like that?" Tabour dazedly inquired.

"Perhaps it was Nora Munday, not you, in whom she was interested."

"According to all accounts Nora was alone on the subway train," Tabour pointed out. "That's why she wasn't identified until the other model saw her in the morgue."

"That's another time, and place, where Zoe Panza opportunely turned up,—for no particular reason," Traherne's reflective voice slid smoothly into the conversation. "What took you to the morgue at that special hour, Miss Panza?"

"I'm afraid I can't quite remember. Visiting it is more or less routine work, you know."

"So?" He dropped the subject and Inspector Fisk put a question to Jerome Tabour.

"You know Hilary Thorp, I think?"

"Eh! Me! Nothing of the kind," Tabour hastily denied. "You can't hook me up with *that* robbery and murder!"

"No? How about the black opal your wife's wearing as an engagement ring?"

Tabour stared incredulously. "What's that got to do with Hilary Thorp?"

"The opal with a fiery green cross in its heart formed a show piece of the Thorp collection."

"Oh my God!" The man's soft white hands went abruptly to his throat, fumbling his collar as if breathing had become suddenly difficult. "And you'll never believe how I came by the stone—it was sent to me, anonymously, through the ordinary mail."

"Hum, doesn't sound especially convincing. It's hardly customary to treat a jewel of that value quite so casually. When did you say you received it?"

"I didn't say, but it was—it was—" Blank horror overspread his face. "Like as not it will help send me to the chair, but it's too late to lie out of it—the damned thing came on the Monday following the Thorp robbery!"

"And you expect us to believe you failed to connect the two events?"

"Never so much as dreamed of a connection," Tabour helplessly insisted, his whole manner revealing that the story sounded incredible even to his own ears. "In the first place the Thorp robbery didn't interest me in the least, I'd scarcely read more than the headlines; and in the second, knowing nothing at all about any precious stones outside of diamonds, it never dawned on me that the thing was valuable. I only thought it was pretty and would look nice on Shirley's hand so had it put into a ring. Why the devil didn't the jeweler who did the job tell me it was worth big money?"

"I suppose he naturally thought you knew. Unfortunately detailed descriptions of the missing stones weren't published—the press was too busy criticizing the police—so he had no reason to suspect he was handling a part of the Thorp collection. Any proof to offer touching your receipt of the opal?"

"No, not a shred!" Tabour groaned.

"Possibly Miss Panza can help." Traherne again emerged from quiescence. "She was better informed concerning the details of the robbery than any one else."

19

"Not better informed than the man who engineered it." Zoe flung him a gayly impudent little smile.

"If it *was* a man," his voice conveyed no more than an impartial interest. "I've always hoped we might sometime catch Zoe in a communicative mood, when she could be persuaded to tell us the parts she's so far left out."

"Why, what outrageous ingratitude—when I've already detailed every inch of the story countless times!"

"Still, there are gaps here and there, both in Slither's version and in yours. Take the vanishing accomplice for example, who, according to Slithers, invisibly melted in and out through the solid walls."

"You can't expect me to know anything about him." The girl reached for a cigarette, lighting it with an air of half bored amusement. "I wasn't there. If you remember I was visiting with you and Inspector Fisk."

"So? And that's another thing I've wondered about. Wasn't Duncan already dead when you left to visit my apartment? The doctors had no chance to examine his body until so long afterward that it wasn't possible to set the precise hour at which he died."

Zoe appeared to carefully weigh the idea before answering. "I can't remember seeing Duncan after dinner was finished so I suppose he might possibly have died while I was in the kitchen with the housekeeper and maid."

"Quite possibly then, or even a little earlier," Traherne agreed. "Of course I quite understood that we owed your visit solely to the fact of having accidentally run into you in the vicinity of the Thorp house only a couple of nights previously."

"Not at all," she flatly contradicted, the tiniest edge of anger in her usually silken voice. "I all along intended passing Slithers' tip to the inspector as soon as Gentsy Judd's plans came to a head."

"Yes? A pity you didn't pass it just a little earlier, say that afternoon. Doing so would have kept you out of an unpleasant, even dangerous situation."

"How do you mean 'dangerous'? I don't in the least understand what you're trying to say!"

"No? Yet it's surely obvious that as things stand at present an unfriendly critic might easily accuse you of a suspiciously close connection with this 'Perfumed Death.' Take its first victim—you were found in the Kenwick house not so very long after Cyril's death and have no explanation to offer regarding how you got inside, how long you'd been there, or how you knew a murder had been committed.

"With its second—little Nora Munday, the description of the unknown lady possessed of a penchant for hiring taxis fits you with surprising closeness; when the lady brought you upstairs tonight she followed my instructions, carefully studying you so that when I questioned her immediately afterwards she was able to tell me you were the woman who had paid her to send Nora to an oculist who promptly disappeared after she had consulted him."

"That's a lie!" Zoe's voice cut sharply across the level flow of his. "I never saw the woman until to-night."

"That I beg leave to doubt, though I'm by no means depending solely on her identification of you as the person who bribed her." He shifted his position so as to include the others as well as the girl sitting almost beside him. "When Nora Munday's body was found on the rear platform of a subway train only one fellow passenger remembered seeing her enter the car at Van Cortlandt Park Station, and he insisted she had come in quite alone. No one else noticed her at all but, as you'll probably remember, the small boy who first drew attention to the tragedy by pointing out to his father how queerly the lady had 'sat down' insisted a girl had come in from the rear platform at 181st street. No one confirmed the child's story, or took it at all seriously, until I became interested in the case, then it seemed to me this story of a second girl deserved investigation. I secured a police list of the subway passengers' names and addresses, hunted up the child's father and minutely questioned the boy himself. He not only seemed to feel very sure that a second girl really had come in from the back platform shortly before Nora was found dead, but declared he would recognize her if he saw her again. That was why I arranged to have the child deliver a dummy letter to-night—he was carefully coached so that while not appearing to do so, he actually studied Zoe and his 'Yes, sir, yes' told me he felt certain she was the girl who got out at 181st street the night of Nora Munday's murder."

Zoe's eyes, so void of expression as to suggest the opaque sheen of inky velvet, were fixed on his face.

"Exactly what are you trying to do?"

"Only to show how plausibly an enemy, or even an unbiased observer, could build up a case against you." Traherne leaned back, his long-fingered hands loosely clasped around one knee. He seemed so unconcerned, so almost indifferent, that Zoe's strained poise also relaxed. She fished in a pocket of her smartly tailored little coat for a cigarette, lighted it, and attempted a fair imitation of her usual curly-lipped smile. Either she did not quite trust her voice or thought silence wisest, for she made no attempt to speak. It was Traherne who broke a pause filled with intangible foreboding.

"And again, on reaching the third murder we find Zoe even more in evidence. We, Inspector Fisk and I, met her one evening on Riverside Drive. Her first impulse was to dodge us, an impulse she conquered, perhaps fearing one of us had already seen and recognized her. After a pleasant little walk and talk Zoe left us to board an uptown bus, but at its first stop I saw her get off, therefore naturally concluded her true destination was below 84th street, not above it.

"Only two nights later she came to my apartment in search of Fisk, whom she wanted to warn that the Thorp house was to be robbed in a couple of hours. Now, dispassionately looked at, the facts might suggest it was Zoe herself who planned the theft of Hilary Thorp's jewel collection. She had entered his service in the assumed character of a maid, won Duncan's confidence so that, according to her own story, he showed her several of the most valuable stones entrusted to his care—among them the very black opal which Tabour claims was afterwards sent him by post—and may, quite conceivably, have confided other secrets such as the combinations of the various wall safes. Probably the original plan didn't include bringing Inspector Fisk on the scene; that was a precaution made advisable by the meeting on Riverside Drive; he might so easily have started wondering why she was close to the Thorp house shortly before it was robbed."

"Why—you're talking almost as if you believed it!" Tabour's puzzled voice slid into a little pause left by Traherne's.

"Oh, dear, no—only trying to be clever!" Something had restored Zoe's self-possession; her infectious chuckle was devoid of the tiniest touch of fear or even nervousness. "Surely you've read enough detective fiction to know he's simply playing Sherlock to our Watsons. Do go on, Mr. Traherne, we're all properly thrilled."

"Enough so to play the game and answer questions?"

"But certainly—you've only to ask."

"A little while back you couldn't remember seeing Duncan after dinner, now, supposing you yourself were the 'cracksman' entertaining designs against the Thorp collection—couldn't you have got the housekeeper and Teddy Thorp out of the way by means of the two faked messages, then rifled the jewel room—supposing its guardian already dead—and chloroformed old Mr. Thorp, all before coming to my house in quest of Inspector Fisk?"

"Oh, yes, that part runs beautifully." Zoe's sleek little head nodded encouragement. "But you're forgetting Teddy Thorp unexpectedly came back and somebody put him out of business. Even your vivid imagination can't picture me as quite big enough to manage that job."

"Not unless he was an assenting party," Traherne acknowledged. "An idea which I suspect the empty chloroform bottle and loosely tied hands were meant to convey. Still, we haven't eliminated Slithers. He was supposed to be stationed in the opposite areaway, carefully watching the house, but we've only his word for the fact, his and yours. Actually, young Thorp may have returned and been welcomed with more skill than tenderness before you ever started for my apartment at all."

"His time schedule was a bit vague," she indifferently conceded. "You've reconstructed what *might* have happened rather well; only a little more and I'll be seeing myself a sort of personified Perfumed Death, trailing round in a melodramatic cape and wide brimmed hat, à la Phantom of the Opera."

"Well, you're good in costume parts." Traherne smiled at her, though the lightness touched only his lips, leaving the oddly striped eyes coldly intent. "Witness your success as the Thorp housemaid and my boy-burglar."

"Eh? What's that about a boy-burglar?" It was the first Conway Fisk had heard of that episode and his interest made him forget the passive role in which Traherne had so carefully coached him.

"That's been our own private secret, but there's no harm in telling it now. You remember the little wicker case we found while searching Hilary Thorp's jewel room? Next day, in your office, you asked if it had confided any secrets and hearing some one outside the door I gave some false information as to its whereabouts for their benefit, not yours. It was Zoe who came in a few seconds later. Up to that time I had no real reason to credit her with more than a reporter's interest in the investigation, but that night I found her, dressed as a boy, hunting my laboratory for the wicker case; of course, she pretended it intrigued her only because of its news value."

"See here, Mr. Traherne, this thing is getting beyond me." There was bewilderment as well as a touch of anger in Jerome Tabour's voice. "I was told you and the inspector'd found enough evidence against me to justify my arrest, but were kindly offering me a chance to privately explain. Now I'm here you turn round and start trotting out damning evidence against Zoe Panza; a lot more of it than you've got against me. What's the idea? Are we supposed to be accomplices, or are you fool enough to suspect any woman of such a daring, cold-blooded series of crimes?"

"Of course, members of the fair sex were never known to indulge in murder," was Traherne's quiet retort. "History and tradition don't show a fairly continuous procession of ladies bearing a fatal poison-cup."

"Oh, well, nobody said women never killed—but a slip of a kid like Zoe, it's ridiculous!"

"Nevertheless it's a trifle singular that the stool-pigeon, Slithers, can tell us nothing of any man principal. All his business, as well as Gentsy Judds, was transacted through Zoe Panza."

"You're getting me more fogged than ever," Tabour aggrievedly protested. "Wasn't it this Slithers who warned Zoe of the cracksman's designs against the Thorp jewels?"

"That's the story given to police and press," Traherne admitted, his eyes never leaving Zoe who had risen with a slightly bored air, moving behind the chair in which she had been sitting to lean her crossed arms on its back as if to place a barrier between herself and the four men. "Gentsy's own story is rather different. He says Slithers approached him with the offer of a sizeable bribe, five thousand to be exact, to earn which he had only to leave the United States for Canada on a specified date."

"The stool-pigeon did that? Then the story of the passed-on tip was a lie?"

"Obviously. Gentsy Judd was simply to be got out of the way and his well-known reputation used to cloak the Thorp robbery. It was probably reasoned that, finding himself suspected of the crime, he wouldn't dare come back and brazen it out."

"And Slithers himself? Who coached him up in the story he told?"

"Zoe."

"Who gave him the bribe for Gentsy Judd?"

"Zoe."

"You mean he never met any male principal at all?" Perplexity lifted Tabour from his chair, sending him prowling heavily about the room. "Then there's this Palmer murder—surely Zoe never entered into that!"

"Well—" Traherne drawled the word, still closely watching. "When the footman first found Lloyd Palmer's body there wasn't any perfume on his lips, though they were strongly scented by the time the medical examiner arrived. Now it's possible to imagine the scent of this mysterious poison only manifests itself some little time after its victim's death—we know too little about it to be sure.

On the other hand, if this strange odor was poured into Palmer's mouth after he was dead—perhaps to disguise the poison's real smell if it was one the doctors would be likely to recognize—only two people are known to have closely approached the body while it was in the car outside the Palmer house. The police who guarded it while Fisk and I interviewed Mrs. Palmer admit letting Zoe lean in at the open window for a close look at the body. Of course, such a procedure was strictly against orders, but she told him she was a reporter, and I think none of us can deny that she's gifted with a dangerously persuasive charm."

"Coming from you that *is* a compliment!" Zoe seemed to be laughing at him, at the entire situation. "But please don't keep us in suspense; who was the other person who leaned in at the car window?"

"Fay Redmond, soon after the body was first discovered."

"*Fay!* I'd forgotten about Fay!" There was a sudden sharp little break in Zoe's voice as both her hands went out in a half defiant, half hopeless gesture—a gesture that was caught and repeated with a sort of exaggerated wildness by her shadow on the window blind. "Am I supposed to be responsible for her disappearance or—death?"

"You've been pretty intimate, just recently, with both Fay and her cousin—I suppose planning the former's abduction would have presented no great difficulty."

"And my motive?" She leaned toward him across the chair-back, a hint of suppressed eagerness in her voice. "Such wholesale murder isn't committed without a terribly strong motive—that is, unless the criminal's a homicidal maniac—"

She stopped abruptly, checked by the sound of running feet which came pounding up the stairs.

"Who's that?" Was it fear, or hope, that pulsed in her whispered question?

The door was flung violently open and Teddy Thorp, very flushed and angry-eyed, stood on the threshold.

"Zoe—? I saw your shadow on the blind, it looked as if you were frightened, so I came up to see what was wrong!"

20

"Nothing, silly boy, everything's as right as rain," Zoe gayly assured him. "I was only being dramatic, and you'd no business watching that window blind anyway; I told you to go on home."

"I couldn't. You put me off and wouldn't explain what was happening here to-night, but I guessed it was something important. After you came inside I started watching all the windows that showed a light—until a few minutes ago nobody came near any of them, then you stood up or moved, so I could see your shadow as you leaned against something, and a bit later a man's shadow struck the blind as he passed between you and the window. Naturally after that I never took my eyes off it—and when I saw you throw out your arms like that I ran up to see if you needed help."

He glared threateningly from one man to the other, evidently quite ready and even anxious to attack whoever gave Zoe the slightest annoyance.

"Goose, we're only having a conference." She administered a half affectionate pat on the boy's shoulder, at the same time trying to gently push him toward the door. "You're interfering, so run along, there's a dear."

"No. I'll stay. There's something going on that I don't understand, and your voice as I came up the stairs didn't sound natural. I only realized it was yours when I got inside and saw you were the only woman here."

"Teddy—" Her great black eyes clung impellingly to his. "You're only making what I have to do doubly hard. Please leave me with my friends."

"But are they?" the boy objected. "They're more like a judge and jury—even the man on the bed hasn't a kindly look."

"He is Howard Munday, whose little daughter was murdered. It's not reasonable to expect him to look happy. Oh, for heaven's sake go!" Her patience suddenly snapped as she caught his gently mulish expression. "We can't waste time explaining and explaining—certain things have got to be settled here and now."

"I'll promise not to interfere, I won't even speak—but I can't leave you alone with them, Zoe, not when I love you as I do."

"Oh, my God, can't you see it's hopeless—haven't I told you I'm not designed for love?" She flung away from him, stopped, and with the same peculiar gesture Traherne had noticed once before, spread out both little hands, fingers stiffly extended, staring down at them with a queer sick horror. A second's silence, and both small hands were thrust boyishly into her coat pockets, while the smooth black head lifted with a brave defiance.

"Have it your own way, then—stay—only don't blame me if you dislike what happens." She swung to face Sydney Traherne, her curly-lipped smile belying the tragedy in her big dark eyes. "Well, the motive—have you found it, Mr. Traherne?"

"We want a confession, Zoe," his voice was oddly pitying, almost tender. "That's what we've been working for."

Teddy's lips opened on a question or protest but the girl seemed able to see all their faces at once.

"You promised not to speak," she curtly reminded him; then, to Traherne, "A confession? Man dear, why should I make your work easier, why—" A sharp spasm contorted her face and was gone. "Why rob you of the glory attached to solving the Mystery of the Perfumed Death?"

At sight of that brief contortion Traherne had sprung from his quietly watchful poise, now he caught her wrists, pulling both tightly clenched hands out of her deep pockets. Zoe offered not the faintest resistance, only smiled at him with a quaintly mournful triumph.

"Zoe!" His cry told of a horror incomprehensible to the others. "I never meant driving you to that!"

"No?" The ghost of her infectious chuckle rose in her throat to die in a tortured gurgle.

"Zoe—there was no need!"

"It's unfair to complain if, now you've cornered me, you don't like the result."

"But why, Zoe girl—why?"

"You wouldn't understand—my mother—" She wavered between his supporting hands, leaning against him as an arm went round her. "Teddy—don't mind, dear my blood is—tainted!"

A convulsion that shook it like a wind-tossed leaf ran through her slender body—they could barely catch the two whispered words:

"My mother—"

The lids fell, veiling the great agonized eyes, and Traherne very gently lowered her to the floor.

"Hold him, Fisk," as young Thorp, overcoming his momentary paralysis of horror, made a forward dash. "He mustn't come near Zoe yet, we want no more deaths; Tabour, hand me that water glass from the dresser."

Both men unquestioningly obeyed him, Fisk holding the half-sobbing Teddy while Jerome Tabour dazedly reached for the water glass. Traherne took it from him, eyes never leaving the girl's face.

"Keep a little back, Tabour—she's almost unconscious—another minute or two—"

As they watched Zoe's tightly curled fingers slowly relaxed, freeing something small and green that had been prisoned in her left hand. It darted toward Jerome Tabour, who instinctively lifted a defensive foot.

"Don't crush it," came Traherne's snapped order. "And for God's sake don't touch it!" His hand shot after the little green fugitive, catching it under the inverted water glass. "It's the Perfumed Death!"

"That? Why it's only a fuzzy green spider!" came Tabour's amazed protest.

"Quite so, and here on the ball of her thumb is the mark where it bit Zoe."

"I can't believe it! Zoe was only a girl, scarcely more than a child." On reading that morning's extra Dr. Munro had straightway rushed down to headquarters, bent on questioning Conway Fisk as to exactly what had occurred. "There must be some mistake!"

"Sydney Traherne seldom makes them, and besides she practically confessed."

"So the papers said. Frankly I didn't believe them. Zoe seemed such a joyous, sweet-natured girl—how could she commit such atrocious crimes?"

"It does sound incredible," the inspector thoughtfully acknowledged. "Yet last night she never once denied her guilt."

"Was she—" Dr. Munro hesitated as if loath to put his question into bald words.

"Insane?" The other did it for him. "No, or at least I think not. She laughed with a gay, sane courage almost to the end."

"Poor little soul." The doctor made no effort to hide his pity. "It's one of the most tragic stories I ever heard. But why did she do it? The papers said nothing at all about her motive."

"You'll have to ask Traherne. I know hardly more than the press has already told you. Last night we had our hands pretty full, what with Zoe's death and young Thorp raging, half mad with grief. Traherne had no time to satisfy my curiosity. He promised to meet me here this morning, but instead I found a phone message saying he'd gone somewhere with Joel Redmond and Jerome Tabour. Probably following a clew touching Fay's whereabouts."

"Fay! I'd forgotten that if Zoe was responsible for those four deaths she must have also had a hand in Fay's disappearance. Didn't she even tell you if Fay is alive or dead?"

"No. Though it's possible that Traherne may know more than I do."

"Forgive me if I say that in my estimation your friend bungled things rather badly. He failed to get anything like an adequate confession and seems no nearer finding Fay than he was before any one suspected Zoe's guilt."

"Wait until you've heard his side before judging," the inspector quietly advised. "He never really airs his conclusions until the last clew has been followed, the last loose end neatly tied. Then he'll light that deep-bowled pipe of his and tell you the 'why' and 'wherefore' with a leisurely clearness that makes you want to kick yourself for not having seen it all from the beginning. He probably knows what motivated Zoe's every action, just as last night he knew there was danger of her committing suicide."

"In that case, why didn't he prevent it?"

"He tried to; I realized afterwards that he never took his eyes off her the whole time we were in Munday's room, but she was too quick for him and too clever an actress. I was there, remember, and the way she thrust both hands into her coat pockets so fitted her normal gayly impudent poise that no one could suspect she'd partly guessed what was coming and brought that hellish spider along."

"It's the first time I ever knew such deadly insects existed. And why didn't it escape from her pocket? The printed accounts were vague on that point."

"The thing was enclosed in a small wicker work case, very similar to one Traherne and I found in the Thorp house," Inspector Fisk explained. "When Zoe decided against facing arrest and subsequent trial she simply opened the case already in her pocket and imprisoned the spider in her hand, holding it, even after the thing had bitten her, until she lost consciousness and her fingers unclosed."

"Horrible!" the doctor muttered. "You must be wrong in thinking she was entirely sane."

"Perhaps—" Here the phone bell shrilled and Fisk took up the instrument. "Inspector Fisk speaking. . . . Oh, that you, Sydney? We were wondering what had become of you. . . . What's that? . . . Oh, the 'we' refers to Dr. Munro and myself, he's here with me now. Are you coming down?"

He listened to the voice speaking over the wire, then turned to Dr. Munro.

"Traherne says he's not feeling well and means staying at home the rest of the day; wants us both to have dinner with him to-night and talk the case over afterwards. There may be one or two other guests. Care to accept?"

"Surely. I'm extremely anxious to know if he has any news about Fay."

"Right . . . Syd, we'll both be there," Fisk again spoke into the phone. "See you at seven then . . . sorry you're not feeling well. Better have a doctor. No? Well, perhaps a good rest is the medicine you need."

When he had put down the instrument he turned back to his companion with a rather worried frown.

"Afraid he's blaming himself for Zoe's death—yet after all it was much the easiest way out for her."

21

During dinner Traherne firmly refused to discuss the case. "First, dwelling on horrors is bad for our digestions, and second, Jerome Tabour is coming in later. I want him present when we dissect actions and motives."

"At least tell me if you've any news of Fay?" Dr. Munro begged, his clear blue eyes darkened by anxiety.

"We know she's alive and perfectly well. That's all I can say at the moment."

"You are telling me the truth?"

"Absolutely, though we've recently seen so much of sudden death that I can't blame you for doubting."

After which Traherne deliberately switched the conversation to an impersonal topic, keeping it to that key throughout the remainder of the meal. The three men adjourned to the study for coffee and were beginning to wonder at Jerome Tabour's tardiness when Traherne's man came in to say Inspector Fisk was wanted on the phone.

"It would be just my luck to be detailed on some new case while I'm hungry to hear Syd's expounding of this one," he disgustedly grumbled. "Fool I was to leave word where I could be found!"

"I've heard Fisk is one of headquarter's best men," Dr. Munro thoughtfully observed, regarding the door through which the inspector's tall figure had just disappeared. "Yet this time he had to call on you for help."

"Perhaps he lost perspective through being too close to the case from its very inception, whereas I only entered it when three consecutive murders, by the same method and presumably by the same hand, had lifted it from the category of what one might term 'personal crimes' into a field requiring wider scope of vision and imagination. Had he first commenced his investigation after the Thorp robbery I doubt if Fisk would have missed the one really essential clew."

"The essential clew!" his guest eagerly repeated. "That's the method of detection advocated by the English Scotland Yard, is it not?"

"Yes, as contrasted to the French insistence on first finding the woman at the heart of every mystery. Here comes Fisk, he sounds as if something had annoyed him."

As a fact the inspector was walking with as near the stamp of an angry child as adult dignity permitted.

"It was Joel Redmond." He picked up his deserted coffee cup and hastily gulped the remainder of its contents. "He's just had a phone message which he's convinced came from Fay, directing him to meet her at a certain spot in Brooklyn. He's determined on keeping the appointment and knowing the somewhat unsavory locality I daren't let him go alone. May bring him back here when he's satisfied that the thing's a hoax, as it undoubtedly is?"

"Of course. Only don't be surprised if we've pretty well thrashed out your Perfumed Death case in the meantime."

"My hard luck." The inspector left them, plainly very much disgruntled by Joel Redmond's inopportune excursion to the uncharted wilderness bordering Brooklyn's more civilized sections.

"You were speaking of an essential clew," the doctor ventured to remind his host as the latter showed signs of becoming unduly absorbed in the proper filling of his favorite briar-root. "Was it one known to the police?"

"To them and to the public at large." Traherne nodded somewhat absent-mindedly. "Its significance simply didn't occur to them, that was all—largely, I think, because they'd watched the gradual unfolding of the death series, studying the details of each case separately, its setting, possible motivation, and particularly the people immediately involved, thereby missing a point of similarity which became apparent once the three murders were regarded not as episodes, but as parts of a single whole."

"You're rousing my curiosity to fever heat," Dr. Munro half ashamedly confessed. "You see, having been called to attend young Cyril Kenwick I was on the ground before even the police. Which fact has added a sharp tang to the interest I should in any event have taken in such an unusual, I might almost say abnormal set of crimes."

"That I quite understand, but speaking personally this spectacular Perfumed Death left me quite cold in the beginning. I happened to be working on a play with particularly intriguing characters and plot, so declined to be divorced from it simply because a not too promising youth and a little dress model had met an untimely end.

"It was only when Zoe Panza unexpectedly turned up here one night, ostensibly to warn Fisk of the contemplated raid on Hilary Thorp's jewel collection, that I was practically driven into taking a hand. After all, three murders inside a week was going it a bit too strong and besides I always did object to poison—it's such a cowardly weapon, leaving the victim without the ghost of a sporting chance.

"Once in the investigation I realized that if all three crimes were engineered by the same brain there must be some overlooked or misread clew pointing to a common motive covering the entire series, and harking back to the death of Cyril Kenwick started searching for it.

"Taking the murders in the order in which they occurred we have, first, a boy whose wildness took a form more injurious to himself than to others. A drunkard, perhaps, or on the road to becoming one and not a particularly useful member of society, still inoffensive enough in the sense that he hardly appeared to be in any one's way. Nobody seemed to possess any strong reason for wishing his removal, except possibly the ex-husband of the woman young Kenwick loved, and in face of the fact that it was Jerome Tabour who divorced Shirley the jealousy-motive failed to carry conviction.

"Second, we have little Nora Munday; by all accounts an inoffensive, hard-working girl, the sole support of her invalid father. Here the murder seemed even more purposeless than Cyril Kenwick's—though again Jerome Tabour entered in as a possibility, having been alone with her during the last few hours of her life.

"Third comes the theft of Hilary Thorp's jewel collection and the death of its guardian. Taken singly the motivation here seemed perfectly simple. The collection was immensely valuable and Duncan, alive, formed a serious obstacle in the path of whoever coveted it, hence his ruthless removal. Had the criminal varied the death method and omitted the rubber band twisted around Duncan's finger this third murder might never have been connected with the two earlier ones.

"The fact that nothing of the sort was done led me to believe that, not only was the acquiring of the jewels no more than a secondary motive behind which loomed some wider design, but that a hint of the latter was intentionally conveyed by the continued use of the same poison and the persistently recurring rubber rings.

"Whether this deliberate linking of the three crimes was done through sheer bravado or for some more subtle reason was at first difficult to decide, so I let the point rest and concentrated on trying to unearth a connection between the various poison victims."

Here Traherne paused, striking a carved Chinese gong on the table beside him. The summons was almost instantly answered by his manservant's entrance with the ingredients necessary for quenching an after-dinner thirst.

"So much talking has made my throat dry as a desert. Joining me, doctor?"

The servant waited while Traherne mixed a drink to his guest's liking and when it had been conveniently placed at the doctor's elbow, asked if anything else was required.

"Nothing else."

"Then, if I shan't be needed, sir, might I go out for a couple of hours?"

"Make it six if you like. I'm expecting some people later on but we can hear the bell from here."

Then, as the man departed with a murmured, "Thank you, sir," Traherne glanced at his watch.

"Queer that Jerome Tabour doesn't put in an appearance. He was supposed to turn up by eight at latest."

"Could he have gone to Brooklyn with the others? This noon the inspector mentioned your being somewhere with both Redmond and Tabour; they may have remained together."

"It's possible for, oddly enough, the two seem to have struck up a kind of friendship, a bit surprising if one remembers how Redmond dislikes Shirley Tabour."

"The Tabours' reconciliation may have softened Redmond's disapproval," the doctor suggested with entire lack of interest, then abruptly returned to the subject that really absorbed him. "You spoke of concentrating on a connection between the three victims—a heavy drinking young spendthrift, a little wholesale dress model, and a staid middle-aged manservant—by what stretch of the imagination can one conceive of their lives ever touching?"

"Stop looking at each case individually and stand far enough away to see them as three prongs of a single fork—then what points of similarity appear?"

"Similarity—why—" The doctor's well-shaped, pliant fingers impatiently ruffled his thickly silvered hair. "The elastic bands found on each dead hand, and, of course, the poison used."

"No other point?"

"Not that I can see."

"There's a third; the essential clew of which I spoke some little time back."

"And that?"

"The presence of an old or elderly man in the very heart of each affair. I admit at first the fact didn't seem to help at all for I had no reason to suppose it would prove any easier to establish a contact between old David Kenwick, Howard Munday, and Hilary Thorp than it had between the immediate poison victims. Still, the three old men were there, and as I don't much believe in coincidence I felt their presence required explanation. A religious fanatic, a bedridden invalid, and a jewel-collecting old recluse—what on earth could they have in common?"

"And in the Thorp case the elderly man in question wasn't related to the murdered man," Dr. Munro pointed out, too absorbed by Traherne's outline of his train of reasoning to realize that he himself was interrupting.

"Quite so. Yet unless we were dealing with an unhinged brain we weren't without at least one guiding clew—those rubber bands meant something. Repeated use of the same lethal method might, just possibly, be because of its proved efficacy, but the rubber bands were simply thrown in gratis, cither from sheer bravado or as a sort of warning.

"Of no intrinsic value and serving no useful purpose—what could they be other than symbols? I'd never heard of any symbolic meaning attached to rubber in itself, even by followers of the Freudian School, and to my own ears it suggested nothing more romantic than footgear and automobile tires, strictly commercial products of our day and age. Commercial? Could the key lie there? Did those baffling rings point to a business contact between the three—a business that had to do with rubber?

"At least the idea was worth following up. I set a research man to work tracing defunct rubber companies, starting with any that had passed out of existence ten years ago and working back from there, for the business activities of all these old gentlemen during the last eight or ten years was already fairly well known.

"In the meantime I myself very thoroughly examined the peculiar little wicker case found in the Thorpe jewel room. Its workmanship suggested some kind of native manufacture, though it was totally unlike anything made by our North American Indians. At the Museum of Natural History they were able to tell me it almost certainly came from South America, though it was slightly different from any specimens known to them.

"When found the case smelled of the exotic perfume we'd come to associate with the mysterious poisoner; of course this odor gradually evaporated but another clew as to how it had been used remained. Inside were a number of infinitesimal green hairs so small they were invisible to the naked eye. Under a powerful glass they looked very much like the tiny hairs that give a bumble bee its fuzzy appearance, so I flew to Chicago and there consulted an old friend who is a famous and much travelled entomologist concerning them. He was able and more than willing to give me some very startling information which I'll pass on in its proper place.

"On getting back to New York I found my research man had unearthed records of a defunct rubber company which had blown up with a scandalous explosion just under twenty years ago. Its directors were six in number, David Kenwick, Howard Munday, Hilary Thorp, Bronson Palmer, Joel Redmond and one other man who has since died."

"And it was actually to this company that the rubber bands pointed?" Dr. Munro was leaning forward, his eyes almost black with excitement. "But Zoe Panza—I doubt she was alive twenty years ago."

"The papers reported the last words she spoke—'My mother'—her motive was a sort of inherited revenge."

"I still don't understand—" The doctor spoke with a touch of dazed bewilderment. "What had Zoe, or her mother, to do with this long extinct rubber company?"

"To answer that question I must go back almost twenty years. At that time the rubber industry was less organized than at present and much less was generally known about rubber trees and their proper cultivation. This group of six men formed a company for the exploitation of South American rubber and sent a youth named Malcolm Gregory to handle their interests in that country. It all happened so long ago that one is unable to judge how well Gregory knew his employers, or whether they confided their ultimate plans to him. All we can be sure of is that the boy, for Malcolm Gregory was very little more, started for Brazil and in due time the company published glowing accounts of the progress he had made there.

"On the strength of Gregory's supposed reports the rubber company sold a tremendous deal of stock, all its directors acquiring tidy fortunes which were snugly tucked away elsewhere before the crash.

"Now the supposed scene of operations was a rubber plantation far up the Amazon—a plantation that reports from Gregory declared to be developing in a manner calculated to make all the company's shareholders wealthy in only a few years' time. Then, quite without warning, some enterprising investigator discovered that a rubber plantation such as the reports described was an impossibility in the part of the country where it was claimed to exist. What Gregory had actually accomplished was to establish a rubber station, not a plantation—a sort of receiving station to which the wild rubber collected by the natives was brought, and afterwards shipped down the river.

"A wild clamor followed the revelation, the company went up in evil-smelling smoke and—Gregory was a disgraced man for the company's directors were able to prove, by documentary evidence, that they were entirely blameless and the whole swindle had been engineered by Gregory acting as their manager and deceiving them quite as much as the general public. He apparently never returned to this country, but people with very long memories tell me he wrote denying the charges made against him, swearing that the reports given out as coming from him were forgeries.

"He evidently lacked evidence or enough money to fight the case and establish his innocence, for after a little the matter dropped and no more was heard of him, but, and this is where Zoe's mother enters in—it came out that young Gregory had been married on the very eve of departure for South America and that his bride was afterwards sent down there at the company's expense; some enemies of the six directors hinting, to prevent her writing her husband, of the inflated stock prices and general misrepresentation of the facts.

"In any case the ship on which young Mrs. Gregory sailed was wrecked after it had started up the Amazon, she fell a prey to unfriendly Indians and was only restored to her husband after undergoing such treatment at their hands that her mind was completely gone. Now do you begin to grasp Zoe's inherited hatred for those six rubber company directors?"

22

The muffled ringing of a distant bell prevented Dr. Munro's immediately answering the question. Instead he glanced at his watch, remarking in a not-too-pleased tone:

"That's probably Jerome Tabour, though he's devilishly late."

"No." Traherne rose without any semblance of haste. "That's the phone, not the door bell. My man must be out by now so I'll have to answer it myself."

While he was gone the doctor sat so wrapped in thought that his cigarette burned down until it scorched his fingers. He dropped it with an impatient grumble and again compared his watch to the clock on the mantel.

"Fisk, calling to say Redmond's car has broken down somewhere in the wilds of Brooklyn and they won't be here for another couple of hours at least," Traherne told him as he came back and resettled for a continuance of their talk. "By the way, you were right about Jerome Tabour, the inspector says he is with them."

"You don't intend waiting for them?"

"No, though it means going over the story twice for up to now I've had no chance to tell Fisk what I've just been telling you."

"You broke off leaving me very much in the air," Dr. Munro feelingly complained. "Is it your idea that Zoe was the daughter of Malcolm Gregory and his unfortunate wife?"

"Of the latter at least—though I'm much less certain of his fatherhood," Traherne gravely responded. "After such a lapse of time we can't do more than hazard a guess as to what happened, but to me it seems a hatred capable of smoldering for almost twenty years and then ruthlessly snuffing out four lives must have been inspired by very terrible wrongs. If those six men not only deliberately ruined his good name, but were also responsible for his wife's falling into the power of natives who tortured and ravished her, thereby destroying her sanity, one can understand that the constant sight of the innocent result of his wife's horrible experience would keep the fires of his hatred burning through almost any number of years. Did you ever happen to notice Zoe's fingernails?"

The doctor only shook an astonished negative.

"While otherwise perfectly groomed she wore the most atrocious liquid nail polish—I believe, that its dark red color might hide the bluish stains so often seen at the base of the nails where the blood is tainted by what we Americans call 'A touch of the tar brush.' She told Teddy Thorp she wasn't designed for love and spoke of tainted blood in connection with her mother. Of course such a theory presupposes black blood, not Indian."

"The whole story is so startling that I can't yet grasp it, and there's one fact that adds to my confusion—if Zoe wanted vengeance on the men who had so terribly harmed her mother, why were none of them killed?"

"It wasn't death they gave to her mother," Traherne quietly pointed out. Nor to the man who occupied a father's usual place in her life. As I see it she reasoned that suffering was the thing they gave, and so tried to repay them in that same coin by depriving each of the thing that was dearest to him. Kenwick of his only son, Howard Munday of his daughter, Hilary Thorp of his beloved jewels which were closer to his heart than any human being. Bronson Palmer loved only his brother, therefore that brother and not he himself was killed, while as to Joel Redmond—I fancy his wife's desertion was the worst that could happen to him."

"Exactly what are you trying to convey?" A strange look was dawning in the doctor's eyes. "Do you know more concerning Fay's disappearance than you've told?"

"Much more. I never for one moment believed that Zoe worked alone and Slithers, as a possible accomplice, was only a cloak to hide the real suspect—her mother's husband, in other words, yourself."

For a second the doctor simply stared at him, then his eyes flashed to the clock on the mantel and back again to Traherne's face.

"You must be mad—" he was beginning, when Traherne's features were suddenly convulsed by an expression of acute agony at sight of which Dr. Munro rose with the swift lithe ease of an animal released from unbearable constriction.

"So at last my little pet strikes!" His laugh rang, triumphantly but coolly sane. "I knew the time limit was almost reached!"

"Then you acknowledge being Malcolm Gregory? Acknowledge responsibility for all four murders?" Traherne demanded, his eyes, had the other stopped to study them, oddly cool considering the pain his face still expressed.

"Surely! No harm in speaking the truth to one so close to death!" came the doctor's answer. "We're alone in the apartment, Fisk and the others aren't due for an hour or more and you've already told me I'm the one person to whom you've confided your suspicions."

"At least you'll admit they were justified—that you are the murderer behind the Perfumed Death?"

"If it's any satisfaction, you're welcome to knowing that all your deductions were substantially correct. From her very cradle Zoe was taught and trained for the part she was meant to play. I knew my repayment could never be worked alone and where else could I have found a tool so perfectly shaped for my handling?

"For long years action was impossible, I hadn't sufficient money—and all that time the sight of my wife, a gentle, mindless thing that cowered with stark terror at the mere sight of a black skin, served to remind me of what she had suffered before her reason broke and kept my hate a living, vital force.

"Then she died and not long afterward money came to me, no matter how. We, Zoe and I, came to New York to settle our reckoning."

He paused, a pained look shadowing his handsome face.

"I never meant that she should be caught and I escape. And it was you who trapped her."

"Yet I no more intended her death than you did. I misjudged her loyalty to you, thinking that when fairly cornered she'd confess everything."

"Since you guessed the real guilt was mine, why did you only try to reach me through Zoe instead of by direct attack?"

"Because the evidence was all against her, not you. At that time you could have laughed at an accusation."

"In that respect the situation hasn't changed a particle." Dr. Munro vented a low, amused chuckle. "While we three drove to the Palmer house the day Lloyd Palmer died, Inspector Fisk betrayed that it was you, not he, who was hot on the poisoner's trail. Since then I've schemed for a chance to eliminate you. It came to-day when Fisk told me you were ill and staying at home."

"Yes, the bait worked nicely," Traherne pleasantly agreed.

"Bait?"

"Quite so. This morning's telephone conversation was carefully prearranged with the idea of getting you to show your hand."

"That's a lie! You couldn't have known I'd be at Fisk's office."

"Do, please, credit us with a bare modicum of intelligence. Zoe Panza's home address was unknown even to the paper that employed her—we reasoned that she might live with you, in which case you'd have known something was wrong when she failed to return from the meeting at Howard Munday's, but even if she lived elsewhere the papers would tell you of her suicide under circumstances making it a practical confession of guilt. What more natural than that you should rush to Inspector Fisk for details of Zoe's death and to learn if you yourself were in any danger? I arranged to phone his office at half hour intervals until one of my calls caught you with him."

"Knowing so much, how did you dare let me prescribe for you to-day? Didn't that boasted intelligence of yours give warning that it was death you swallowed?"

"A risk taken in the cause of justice. Remember that while sure of your guilt I had next to no proof, so was obliged to try and trick you into supplying some. We arranged to let you consider me your only real danger and then Fisk casually told you I was sick and spending the afternoon at home; your call to offer friendly medical advice was almost a foregone conclusion."

"Then—you deliberately took that capsule—?"

"Knowing what it contained? Yes. And the instant you'd gone employed a stomach-pump, in the presence of half a dozen unimpeachable witnesses."

"But your spasm of pain just now?"

"Was timed to fit your evident expectations—you showed rather too keen an interest in my mantel clock—I guessed that when you thought my dying only a question of minutes you'd be apt to speak freely, admitting a guilt we'd have hard work to bring home without your own unqualified confession."

Traherne's voice was so tranquilly matter of fact that it seemed to leave no room for emotional outbursts of either rage or despair, and Dr. Munro's manner kept to the same detached, almost impersonal level.

"After all it amounts to no more than your word against mine." He took out another cigarette and, lighting it with steady fingers, sat down on the arm of a big chair, one long leg casually a-swing across the other. "You claim I confessed to all four murders—I deny doing anything of the kind—we're quite alone here and I hardly think a jury would accept your unsupported word."

Then, as Traherne remained quietly intent on the refilling of his pipe, Munro went on speaking, still with the impartial air of a person discussing some altogether theoretical problem.

"Our plans were so carefully laid, Zoe's and mine, so patiently carried out, I'm still wondering how you guessed."

Instead of answering, Traherne in turn put a question. "Why did you wait so long before striking the first blow?"

"Mainly that I might acquire a background of impeccable respectability and Zoe have time to establish herself as an ambitious girl-reporter specializing on crime news—to whom the police were so accustomed that they'd never dream of connecting her with a series of spectacular crimes. Also a good deal of preliminary work had to be done if we wanted to avoid making slips.

"Luckily the five surviving company directors all lived in New York and all but Howard Munday were prominent enough to be easily found; with him we had some little trouble but ran him to earth in the end. None of them would know me, I was sure of that; twenty years alters any man past casual recognition and I barely met the directors at the time their business manager engaged me for the South American post. Still it was safer to gain all the necessary data concerning their lives, families, affections, without personally meeting any of the five and it all took time."

"Did you actually study medicine, or was that only a blind?"

"Rather more than that, though I've no actual diploma. I read and studied enough to pass muster even with a physician. You'll have to admit the whole scheme was prettily worked out. I'm still wondering just what put you on the right track."

"Zoe. She was clever, but even her winsome impudence couldn't hide her always turning up so near the murder before she'd any legitimate right to know there was one. Inspector Fisk explained it by a leak at headquarters—I by foreknowledge."

"Dangerous of course, but unavoidable. One of us had to be near the body."

They were both speaking as though the matter held only an academic interest, not imprisonment and almost certain death for the man who sat serenely smoking, still lightly perched on the chair-arm.

"Your idea was to trade on the terror of the unknown, believing it would help to obscure the real method?"

"Not only that, the spiders are individual to the Amazon country, found nowhere else in the world, and I didn't want the poison localized. I'd lived too long, and was known too well in that particular region. Just how much did your friend the entomologist read from the little green hairs?"

23

"With only those little green hairs as a guide he could hardly make a very definite statement. He told me of a weird green variant of the pitcher plant which he'd once seen when traveling many miles up the Amazon on one of his periodical bug hunts. Like others of its kind the plant was designed as a natural trap, always partially filled with a watery liquid into which unlucky insects lighting on its lip were bound to fall, as the throat of the pitcher-shaped blossom was lined with stiff, down-pointing hairs which prevented their escaping once they were fairly inside.

"With the uncanny adaptability common to most of the spider species, a certain venomous spider of the region either originally green in color or become so in order to better match their habitat, had become parasites on these pitcher plants living inside them and taking toll of the insect prey designed for the plant's own use.

"These horrible little creatures were so deadly that the natives paid them a kind of semi-religious homage, laying propitiatory offerings on the lip of the pitcher plant with a muttered prayer that its inhabitant might remain permanently inside.

"My friend believed that the green hairs I showed him had come from one of these pitcher plant spiders, the more so because the wicker case in which they were found was unmistakably of Brazilian manufacture.

"Yet even with such knowledge of the poison used the question, How was it possible for one of these deadly spiders to bite and leave its victim unmarked by any sign which the doctors could discover? remained unanswered. It was only when Constance Palmer told me about the herb doctor's cure for alcoholism, and described the capsule he'd sent her and which her unsuspecting husband had duly swallowed, that I realized the devilish cleverness of your method. You simply enclosed a living pitcher plant spider in a capsule that would take from three to four hours to dissolve and release its prisoner—when that happened the spider struggled to work its way upward toward the mouth and freedom, and during the passage inflicted a death-bite at some point inside the victim's body, where the doctors would never dream of looking for the much talked of puncture. Thus the venom became mixed with the blood, as in the case of an ordinary injection, while the stomach contents showed no trace of poison. Is it any wonder the doctors were puzzled?

"But had the spider been left inside the body all mystery touching the exact cause of death would have instantly vanished, and suspicion turned toward some one who knew the Amazon country. You therefore safeguarded yourself and added a touch of bizarre mystery by enticing the spider out through the mouth of the body by means of a perfume which irresistibly attracted it."

"The distilled essence of the pitcher plant's own fragrance," Munro put in helpfully. "But I still don't understand how you traced my little pets' activities to me."

"Zoe's part was fairly obvious, for once Lloyd Palmer's body was found with an unscented mouth to which the perfume was later added I knew it as an aftermath of the victim's death, not its cause. Remembering Zoe's persistent closeness to each murder I reasoned that it was she who recaptured the spiders after their deadly work was accomplished, and naturally guessed an association between her and the actual murderer. It seemed most logical to examine anyone who insistently cropped up in the case before canvassing the world at large. Jerome Tabour rather played the part of a red herring and confused the trail, but I never seriously suspected him."

"Then the scene at Howard Munday's was only a stage set?"

"No more. We wanted to get Zoe there without rousing her suspicions. It was the easiest place into which to bring both the landlady and the small witness from the subway train; both of whom identified her, as you know. I thought she'd confess when directly accused, but she died without once mentioning your name."

"Then why select me as her accomplice?"

"Hardly that," Traherne gravely reproached him. "The child was your tool, on whose mind you'd stamped this vengeful hate of yours from her very infancy. Personally I think that in thus twisting her nature awry you committed a worse crime than even in dealing out such wholesale death. But putting that phase aside—once I got the case into proper perspective I realized you were one of the few who entered more than one group of the people involved, that fact necessitated inquiry into your life and general background, I found your first appearance in New York coincided with Zoe Panza's, she appeared in the newspaper world two years ago, you bought the house a few doors from David Kenwick's at about the same time.

"Your theory touching the similarity between man- and beast-hunting told me you'd lived in wild places. Your skin had the sallow pallor of a brunette's who has lived long in the tropics, and the envelope of Constance Palmer's from the herb doctor showed it had been mailed at a Post

Office Station in the vicinity of your home. Then I found that both Nora Munday and Duncan were ill some little time before their deaths and, with the idea of discovering the state of Cyril Kenwick's health, I consulted his family doctor. From him I learned that the butler, Barnabus, lied in saying he was out of town the night young Kenwick died—and with that knowledge in my possession was able to force Barnabus into confessing that several weeks before the first murder you'd scraped a neighborly acquaintance with him and obtained his promise to send for you instead of their regular physician the next time any one in the house was ill. The promise cost you a stiff price but was worth it, as its fulfillment gave you a semi-official entry into the case.

"As I see it, you yourself enticed the spider out of young Kenwick's body so it could be recaptured—I know you were left alone with the corpse while Barnabus saw to the comfort of the old man who awaited the police in another room—while Zoe used the perfume on the three subsequent victims. Am I correct in supposing that when the capsule enclosing the spider melted, the latter escaped destruction by the gastric juices because of a certain similarity between their chemical action and that of the liquid filling the pitcher plant in which it habitually lived?"

"Quite correct. I tried the experiment with several animals and one native before finally shaping my plan of action, and in each instance it was perfectly successful—the patient died in from three to four hours. Since they say confession is good for the soul I'll fill in what lapses you've left." Munro began sauntering aimlessly around the room while he talked. "Taking them in proper order I'll explain how the various selected victims came to swallow my little pets. Understand we were keeping close track of them all, and having often watched Cyril's hilarious homecoming in the wee small hours, I knew such persistent drinking could hardly fail to impair his health.

"Living so close, it was an easy matter to scrape acquaintance. I casually mentioned the evils consequent on too free indulgence in prohibition liquor and, when he complained of certain ill effects, offered to prescribe for him. That last Sunday he stopped at my office on his way home from the park, I administered a so-called antidote for the symptoms described—after which his death was a foregone conclusion.

"With Nora Munday we found she suffered from eye strain—Zoe bribed her landlady into sending her a certain oculist—and in that character I simply waited until she came to the office I'd rented for the purpose. Knowing that if she died in the wholesale dress factory it would be extremely difficult to get near her body, I told Nora to take the prescribed pill after dinner that night. She seriously complicated matters by choosing that particular evening for a prolonged joyride with Jerome Tabour, but since our policy was always to keep as near the victim as possible during the critical hours and we couldn't be sure the girl would go directly home, Zoe was on watch outside the building where Nora worked so when she came out and joined Tabour, was able to follow in a taxi. The rest of that episode is also known to you, I think."

"Quite." Traherne's brindled head nodded, as he divided his attention between his pipe, which for some reason refused to draw properly, and the still slowly prowling Munro.

"With Hilary Thorp I at first planned killing his nephew, but more intimate knowledge of the man taught me his jewel collection lay infinitely closer to his heart—so my plan was shifted to deprive him of that instead. It was Zoe who talked to Duncan about the indigestion from which he suffered and sent him to her own physician. You were quite right in thinking he was already dead, Hilary Thorp chloroformed and the jewels removed from the house before Zoe left it to find Conway Fisk. Of course it was I who put Teddy Thorp out of commission. I'd stayed in the house on the chance of his coming back too soon."

Munro stopped near the window, letting up the shade so that he could look out at the city's twinkling lights; thereby turning his back squarely toward his still seated host.

"The details of the Palmer affair you've discovered for yourself—which settles four of the directors. The fifth, Joel Redmond—"

He turned from the window, resuming his restless prowl which carried him close to Traherne, who seemed still preoccupied with his restive pipe.

"How much have you guessed concerning his wife?"

His leisurely saunter had taken him past Traherne's chair and across toward the rear wall of the long room. As he turned for the return trip Traherne held his refractory pipe up against the light, squinting at it as if trying to discover what was wrong. Munro's right hand was suddenly raised and what looked like a small green ball shot through the air to land in the big chair from which a swift sideways leap had lifted Traherne only a second before. He whirled to face Munro, still poised with right hand in air.

"Better recapture your little pet." Traherne glanced from the spider which, following the custom of its kind when frightened, remained curled into a harmless looking ball, to the thick rubber glove Munro had drawn on while standing at the window. "Or no, on second thought it will be safer so." He inverted an ash receiver over the still inert spider. "Stupid move. Why make the average criminal's mistake and underestimate your opponent?"

"I'd no reason to suppose you wore eyes in the back of your head." The anger undernoting Munro's chagrined laugh was directed more against himself than Traherne. "Call it an example of mental telepathy or what women describe as intuition?"

"Nothing so high sounding. Simply a polished bloodstone ring held so the light struck it at an angle, reflecting what went on behind me. You were speaking of Fay Redmond—where is she, by the way?"

The question was casually put but it brought Munro up short; he stared for a second, then laughed again.

"So that's one thing you haven't found out?"

"No. Otherwise our talk would have been slightly less prolonged."

"I see, you hoped I'd drop a hint of her whereabouts without any direct question. Offering any inducement?"

"Not necessary. Fay'll come forward of her own accord once she hears of your arrest."

"Ah, but suppose she doesn't hear?" Munro pleasantly inquired. "If I decide on making her a fifth victim of the so-called Perfumed Death, won't you feel her extinction heavy on your conscience?"

"You'll have no opportunity. After your extremely plain speaking we'd scarcely be such fools as to let you leave here—a free man."

"We?" Munro's dark brows climbed to a quizzical arch. "So far the matter lies between you and me, and, speaking of fools—do you seriously imagine I intend letting you live to repeat our confidential talk?"

"The choice hardly lies with you." Traherne strolled nearer to the center table. "And, remembering Teddy Thorp's account of your skill in jujitsu, I see no point in risking a broken arm or leg, not to mention a quite possible neck."

Before the other guessed his intention he had struck the Chinese gong a quick, light blow, in almost instant response to which the room's two doors opened; one framing Conway Fisk against a background of plain-clothes and uniformed figures, a vicious looking automatic casually dangling from his thumb; the other Joel Redmond, lean, distinguished, with Bronson Palmer's drink-ravished face, and David Renwick's vulture-head peering one over either shoulder.

For a second Alan Munro stared from one group to the other, then, ignoring Fisk and his men, bowed to the three in the opposite doorway with his own inimitable grace.

"So—we meet again, but with three of your number missing, one worm's food these many years, one bedridden, I regret to say through no act of mine, one still confined to his bed weakly whimpering for his lost jewels, which it deeply grieves me to know will be restored to him when my country home is found and searched."

So strong was the man's personality, so oddly fascinating his poise of malicious triumph, that they listened, no one attempting to interfere.

"Sad, is it not, to have nursed my hate through the years, plotted and schemed full repayment, and then to have failed in exacting it from two of the men who destroyed my youth! Kenwick cared nothing for the loss of his only son! Realizing that fact was a bitter disappointment and one I could do nothing to alleviate, for the only thing close to his heart is a strange, warped version of the Christian God—something of which it's impossible to deprive him. And Hilary Thorp, he'll regain his lost happiness with his jewels."

"Where are they? Where is Fay?"

It was Joel Redmond, driven by desperate fear for the wife he so loved, who finally broke the spell of inaction that had claimed them all. Munro turned to him, splendid eyes mockingly a-glitter.

"She is in my second home, which also shelters growing specimens of the Amazon pitcher plant and its deadly little parasites. Only evil chance can bring Fay within their reach, still with a woman one can never be sure—knowing how I value them and quite unaware of their deadly attributes, she may think when I fail to return home that they need attention and go too close."

"You've dared imprison her in such a place?"

"Imprison? Far from that. Fay came to me and *stayed,* quite of her own free will."

"Liar!" Redmond's features were convulsed with fury. "You kidnaped her!"

"Not at all, I simply won her love, feeling that you'd infinitely prefer losing her to death's arms than to mine."

"No!" The sharp command came from Traherne, who had caught Redmond's shoulder in time to prevent his attack on the man who mocked him. "A physical brawl will do no good and while Fay remains in the same house with those insects there's danger of some accident occurring. Munro—"

He faced their prisoner with quiet authority.

"To-night's trap was set down to the minutest details—concealed dictographs have recorded your every word—Conway Fisk, who never left the apartment at all, and these three gentlemen have listened by means of dictaphones. In face of such overwhelming evidence against you your fate is practically sealed—why risk adding another death to the already appalling list? Why not tell us where Fay is?"

"Shall I?" Munro asked himself, a hint of softness dimming the glittering excitement in his eyes. "Shall I? As you say, my own fate is sealed and nothing can now undo what has been or give Joel Redmond back his lost happiness. After all I've no grudge against Fay herself, indeed if twenty years ago these men hadn't slain all capacity for human tenderness, I might even have given her real love instead of counterfeit."

He quietly gave Traherne explicit directions how to reach his cottage tucked away on Long Island.

"Caring nothing yourself, you deliberately tricked my wife into loving you for the sole purpose of making me suffer?" With the usual partiality of those who love, Joel Redmond seemed unable to credit the other's indifference to Fay's supreme charm.

"Just as deliberately as you, years ago, connived at sending mine to a country unfit for any white woman," Munro's voice held a sudden venomous snarl. "True, you and the others had no actual hand in her trans-shipment to an upriver boat, a rotten tub unable to weather even an inland storm and captained by a drunken brute who let her fall into native hands—but the true responsibility was yours. Did none of you guess the meaning of those rubber bands twisted round the third finger of each dead hand I added to the count? I meant them as a reminder to those who had sent my wife on a journey ending in outrage and badness, a reminder and a veiled threat which I knew couldn't pass on without at the same time revealing your own knavery and my reason for seeking vengeance."

While he talked Munro had been constantly edging closer to the chair in the broad seat of which lay an untidy ash tray, upside down. Only he and Traherne knew what it hid; to the rest, if they noticed it at all, the ash tray meant no more than a sign of some one's carelessness.

He reached the chair, leant lazily against its back, still holding them with a flow of words that to his own ears had ceased to matter, while his eyes sought Traherne's. If ever human eyes held entreaty, compelling demand, a desperate plea for escape, his did and Traherne, reading their message, knew that if he let that strong, sensitive hand right the ash tray it would bode no harm to any other in the room.

The man was a criminal, a four-time murderer, yet he had already greatly suffered—was not the simpler, quicker atonement the better way?

Slowly, deliberately, Traherne answered those imploring eyes by turning away and walking to the window.

The Hollow Tree Mystery
MADELON ST. DENIS

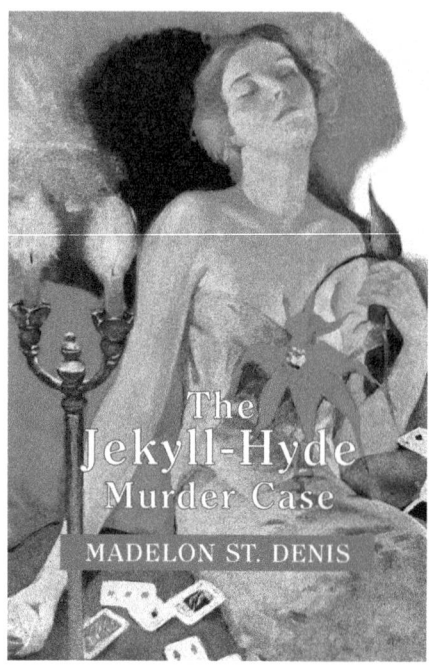

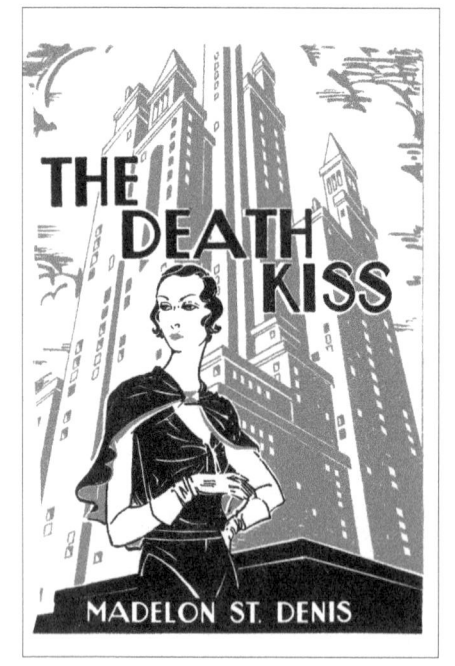

The Jekyll-Hyde Murder Case
MADELON ST. DENIS

THE DEATH KISS
MADELON ST. DENIS

The MURDERS AT HILLSIDE
VIRGINIA RATH

Coachwhip Publications
CoachwhipBooks.com

Coachwhip Publications
CoachwhipBooks.com

THE FIRES AT FITCH'S FOLLY
KENNETH WHIPPLE

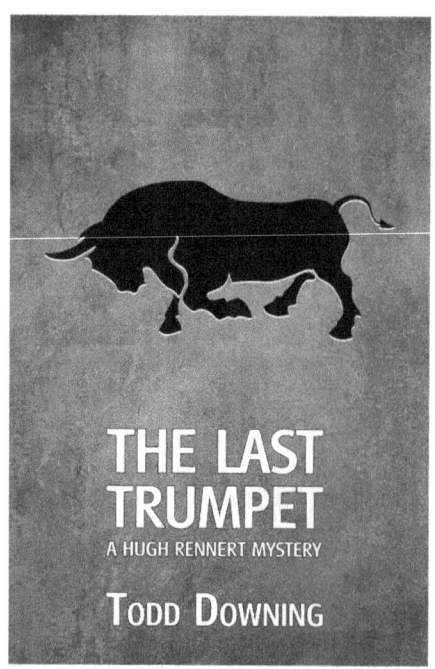

THE LAST TRUMPET
A HUGH RENNERT MYSTERY
TODD DOWNING

Jack Dolph
MURDER MAKES THE MARE GO

BLOOD-RED DEATH
MINNA BARDON

Coachwhip Publications
CoachwhipBooks.com

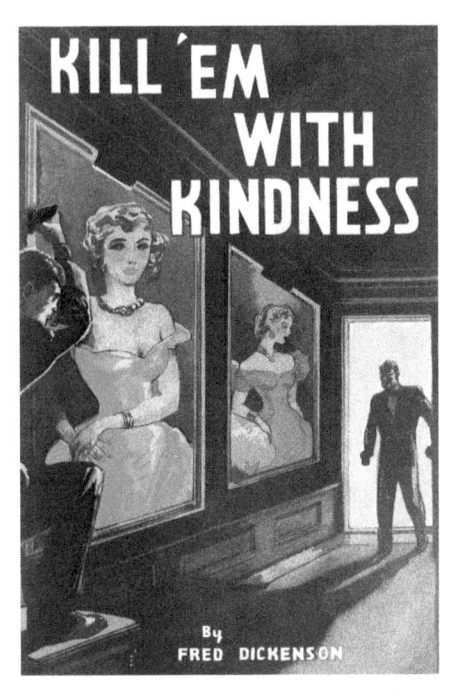

KILL 'EM WITH KINDNESS
By FRED DICKENSON

LADY IN LILAC
SUSANNAH SHANE

The Railroad Murder Case
R. M. LAURENSON

A SULTAN'S HAREM MYSTERY
Drink the Green Water
The Milkmaid's Millions
HUGH AUSTIN

Coachwhip Publications
CoachwhipBooks.com

LOUIS F. BOOTH
THE BANK VAULT MYSTERY
BROKERS' END

MURDER IN THE FAMILY
NICE PEOPLE MURDER
Mary Hastings Bradley

BLOOD ON HER SHOE
MEDORA FIELD

MURDER AT DRAKE'S ANCHORAGE
E. LEE WADDELL

Coachwhip Publications
CoachwhipBooks.com

Coachwhip Publications
CoachwhipBooks.com

Printed in the USA
CPSIA information can be obtained
at www.ICGtesting.com
CBHW030541160724
11654CB00008B/99